CI
OF
DREAMS

Pranaya SJB Rana is sometimes a writer, sometimes an editor, oftentimes both. He has worked as a journalist and editor for *The Kathmandu Post* and *Nepali Times*. He lives in Kathmandu and listens to hip hop.

CITY
OF
DREAMS
STORIES

Pranaya SJB Rana

RUPA

Published by
Rupa Publications India Pvt. Ltd 2015
7/16, Ansari Road, Daryaganj
New Delhi 110002

Sales centres:
Allahabad Bengaluru Chennai
Hyderabad Jaipur Kathmandu
Kolkata Mumbai

ISBN: 978-81-291-3728-9

Second impression 2016

10 9 8 7 6 5 4 3 2

The moral right of the author has been asserted.

Typeset in Adobe Jenson pro by SŪRYA, New Delhi
Printed at Shree Maitrey Printech Pvt. Ltd., Noida

For my mother

'…Cities, like dreams, are made of desires and fears, even if the thread of their discourse is secret, their rules are absurd, their perspectives deceitful, and everything conceals something else.'

'I have neither desires nor fears,' The Khan declared, 'and my dreams are composed either by my mind or by chance.'

'Cities also believe they are the work of the mind or of chance, but neither the one or the other suffices to hold up their walls. You take delight not in a city's seven or seventy wonders, but in the answer it gives to a question of yours.'

'Or the question it asks you, forcing you to answer, like Thebes through the mouth of the Sphinx.'

—Italo Calvino, *Invisible Cities*

Contents

City of Dreams

Kanti grew up in the middle of Kathmandu, in a two-storey brick house with wrought iron windows. When young, he played marbles in the alleys of Lazimpat with the boys from the neighbourhood. Eventually, Kanti developed an uncanny aim, able to hit a marble the size of a pea from five long steps away. It was luck, his friends always complained, but Kanti knew it was something more than that. He was gifted.

The belief that there was something special about him solidified when his mother took him to Asan for the first time. He was six then and had just been accepted into Class 1 at the Guheswari English Medium School. In Asan, they were to fit Kanti with two sets of school uniforms—navy blue pants with a crisp white shirt. He would wear one set for three days and the second set for two. The school itself would provide a striped red tie for a one-time cost of 150 rupees. In the winter, he would be allowed a navy blue sweater and a navy blue blazer. But sweaters and blazers cost more money, so for now they were in Asan only to get shirts and pants.

Kanti was walking beside his mother but not holding her hand because he had started school now. She led him through the labyrinth of Asan's streets with an ease honed by years of

familiarity. After all, she was a Kathmandu Newar, birthed
and broken in the gallis of Jhonchhe. Asan, with its warren of
alleyways, its narrow matchbox buildings that blotted out the
sun, and a thousand bodies bustling to and fro, was her
backyard. Kanti's mother weaved through people, never once
bumping into anyone. Kanti tried to keep pace but he was
small and people often didn't see him. He was jostled by
purses, backpacks, umbrellas and bicycles. But it didn't bother
him any. Kanti was used to such adventures. Besides, he
wasn't bumping into people, *people* were bumping into him.

It was only when his mother slipped into a sari store that
Kanti lost sight of her. He had been following closely but had
been forced to slow down after spying some Nagraj comics on
display. He didn't dare go up to the store, so he slowed his
pace, squinted his eyes and tried to make out just which villain
Nagraj was beating up this time. To his utter astonishment,
Nagraj was actually being beaten by none other than machine-
gun toting, dog-mask-wearing vigilante crime-fighter, Doga.
By the time Kanti had finished ogling, his mother had vanished.
Unperturbed, he continued to walk, passing the very store she
was in, and slipped into Asan chowk where five stone-paved
roads and a number of smaller pathways fed into one large
courtyard teeming with people. Kanti picked a lane and
trundled along, peering between people for the sea-blue kurta
his mother was wearing. Neither the fact that he had lost his
mother nor his not knowing where he was going bothered
him. He was content exploring the city. The air was pungent
with the smell of spices and there were all kinds of men and
women about. He even spied a sadhu baba, naked except for a

maroon loincloth, holding out a metal canister for rice and money. He wished he had something to give so that he could receive a long vermillion tika in return.

He had sauntered for close to fifteen minutes and had almost reached New Road when he decided to turn back. Although he was enjoying the walk immensely, he knew his mother would be worried. He strode quickly on the way back because he had already seen most of the interesting bits. He almost reached the stationery store with the comic books when he saw his mother, frantically searching this way and that for him. She looked harried, her hair was coming loose from its ponytail and her purse hung limply from one slumped shoulder. When she saw him, she ran to him, slapped him across the face and twisted his ear. Kanti didn't cry or say anything. He knew he shouldn't have wandered off. All the way to the uniform tailor, his mother scolded him for his transgression. Kanti listened to her rebukes with one stinging ear, nursing one red cheek. He had answers to all her rhetorical questions, but chose to keep quiet to avoid aggravating her further. So she went on—what if she had never found him? What if he had been kidnapped? What if he had got lost?

If only she knew—she wouldn't have had to find him; he would've found her.

By the time Kanti secured his school leaving certificate in Class 10, he had explored almost every road, galli and nook of Central Kathmandu. From the five-star hotels of Lazimpat, the spacious old-world walled compounds of Bishalnagar, the urban sprawl that is Dhumbarahi, and the nondescript Battisputali, to the messy, dirty, pungent Bagbazaar, the chaos of New Road, and the madness of Asan, back home to Lazimpat—Kanti considered all this Kathmandu proper, his own Kathmandu, and he walked it like an explorer, a cartographer, a preserver even. He ducked into alleys that turned into roads, into doorways that opened up into courtyards. He traced new pathways through empty lots and negotiated the tops of low brick walls. He cut across front yards and snuck through backyards. He climbed trees and jumped fences. He avoided wide roads and squeezed sideways in between houses built too close. He knew to keep the setting sun to his left and the far-off hill with the conspicuously naked rocky outcropping to his right. And, despite the fact that he rarely took the same path twice, he always knew, as if by instinct, which path led where.

After Class 10, Kanti joined a new high school in the northwestern end of Kathmandu Valley, along the Ring Road. It was some distance from his home but the walk to and fro was always the best part of his day. He left home at eight in the morning, committed to an hour's brisk march; the new pathways he discovered were often strange and sometimes dangerous. Once, two boys, barely older than him, eyes red and speech slurred, asked him for a hundred rupees. When he said that he didn't have the money, they pushed him down and punched him in the face twice before filching the fifty rupees he had in his pockets. The punches had been weak, and except for Kanti's ego, nothing was severely hurt. Another time, a skinny, scraggly mutt with a broken ear chased him for nearly ten minutes. Kanti had dealt with dogs before. Usually, a stamp of the foot was enough to send them off, but this one was especially difficult. Soon Kanti was running, his backpack clutched tight against his body and the dog snapping at the heels of his black school shoes. Eventually, Kanti managed to hop on to a wall high enough to keep the dog out. Since then he avoided those two particular paths.

At school—and later, college—Kanti's male friends had motorbikes and a number of his female friends had scooters. Those who didn't had girlfriends and boyfriends who did. The few who rode the bus and microbus were seen as straitlaced and gently ridiculed. But no one walked like Kanti did. His classmates thought him eccentric and tried to give him rides. He always refused, politely but firmly. When it rained, he carried an umbrella and arrived home with his shoes full of water and his pants dripping.

Of course, these long walks in relative silence did little to quell neighborhood rumours about that strange 'hidirakhne keto', the boy who walks. Onlookers would see him wandering and wonder just where it was he was going to and where he was coming from. They wondered why he didn't ride the microbus or buy a motorbike like most boys his age and of his standing. After all, his parents—one an engineer and another a nurse—weren't exactly poor.

Kanti's parents, naturally, were worried. They took him to see a jyotish in Bagbazaar during his first year of college, when his daily wanderings showed no signs of stopping. The jyotish was a middle-aged Brahmin with a paunch and a long saffron tika on his forehead. He wore cotton pants and a cotton shirt, no dhoti like Kanti had imagined. He perused Kanti's cheena, noted down his birth day, month, year and hour. He repeated Kanti's name out loud five times while making calculations on a scrap of paper. Then he looked up and announced that since Mangalgraha, or Mars, was in an unbeneficial quadrant with Sunny, or Saturn, things did not look too good. A puja would have to be performed. In the meantime, he would give Kanti a herb packed into a little pouch to wear around his neck. This would kill his desire to go wandering.

The parents left the jyotish's relieved. But the very next day, Kanti was walking to school; he even started returning home later than usual.

Eventually, Kanti secured a job. It wasn't anything special but it was one that his father's close friend had got especially for him. So he did the best he could—the same thing every day, just like the ten or so people who worked around him. He filed, copied, stamped and signatured. He passed on and was passed up. He talked little and laughed even less, again earning a reputation as a strange one. Women seemed oddly attracted to him and often took the effort to solicit his attention, whether he replied favourably or not. In any case, he wasn't particularly interested in women, nor did he care much for the company of men; he already had a paramour of his own.

Kanti ate his lunch in the office canteen, sitting by himself and always in a corner. He brought his food from home, which his mother packed in a neat metal tiffin box. Usually, his lunch consisted of four rotis and one vegetable tarkari, with chicken every Monday and fish every Friday. He ate fast, rolling up the vegetables or meat in his roti and eating it in three large bites. He then spent the rest of his hour-long break exploring the city. His office, located on the fifth floor of a shiny new concrete building with a glass façade, was in Baneshwor, all of which he surveyed within a few months. After that, he started riding a bus, any bus, in a random direction, travelling until he reached somewhere he had never been before, and then getting off. He'd then find a path back to his office.

Kanti couldn't jump across walls and climb trees like he used to anymore but he found that new roads were always open to the enterprising. An air of self-importance could get you into any building in the city, he discovered. So he began to dress better—tailoring a suit in a clean, sweet-smelling shop in Durbar Marg; keeping his hair always neatly parted to the side; and ensuring that his face remained free of any unsightly stubble. He polished his shoes blindingly bright and pressed his tie stiff each morning. He ate well, and never drank nor smoked. So when he walked into offices, restaurants and private homes in his quest for a new path, he looked like he was there for a reason. No one stopped this man who barely spoke—or spoke in short, steady bursts when trespassing gated homes—but who always walked with an air of confidence and smiled at everyone who met his gaze. Besides, he left as fast he could, quickly scoping out an exit—a kitchen door, a back door, a side door—through the building instead of around it. If no one was around, he'd slip out of windows.

Buildings, roads and bridges made up the city, Kanti knew that. So did trees, rivers and hills. But he had never quite thought about people. He was told that that they, too, were integral parts of a metropolis; if Kathmandu were an organism, people were its red blood cells, navigating busily through road-veins and street-arteries. But Kanti didn't welcome humanity's presence. To him, people were appendages, vestigial organs that had served their purpose. The fact remained—in every social situation, Kanti always felt like he did not belong. Among people, he was truly lost.

Once, he walked into a narrow alley in between two bhattis where three teenage boys were smoking ganja and passing around a half-bottle of cheap whisky. They hastily stepped on the joint and hid the bottle behind their backs when they saw him and his suit. But Kanti simply smiled at them and deftly squeezed through a crevice in the wall they were leaning against. Another time, he walked down a dark first-floor corridor of one of the hundreds of massage parlours in Thamel and, inside a side room with a curtain for a door, saw a clothed man and a naked woman on a rickety cot in an amorous embrace. The woman screamed and the man cursed when they saw a suited gentleman looking in.

Kanti met, or rather surveyed, all kinds of people during his travels. Most people he saw but once. They were blurs, shadow people in a city alive. But some he found intriguing—like an unexpected modern anomaly on a fifteenth century temple dabali in Basantapur, they surprised him. He chanced upon two hairdressers kissing behind a black water tank, each with a cigarette in his hand. He saw a young kid, barely fifteen, selling brown sugar to an older kid, barely twenty, who was swaying on his feet. He walked into a studio space, in the middle of a photo shoot, and saw the most beautiful girl he had ever laid eyes on. She was standing stark against a dazzling white background as three high-powered lights shone down. She had an oversized floppy hat on her head and a short Chinese dress that showed off her legs all the way to her thighs. She had spotted Kanti and, instead of being annoyed at being interrupted, she had smiled, a tiny mole by the side of her lips rising with the corners of her mouth. Kanti left the studio the way he had entered it, predictably shaken out of his confidence by a beautiful woman. Another day he heard, through the thin walls of a rented room, a couple breaking up, the man's voice trembling and sorrowful and the woman's steady and callous—no, she hadn't found another man, she just didn't like him anymore.

Over time, Kanti passed by grieving corpse-bearers, revelling groomsmen, jaunty bikers at motorcycle rallies, strike enforcers, citizen protestors, armed policemen, political leaders, British Gurkha hopefuls, women's rights activists and Hindu-nation fanatics.

Kanti knew that he was not one of these people. To them, the city was just the streets they walked and the buildings they entered. To Kanti, Kathmandu was something infinitely more. This city—at once vibrant and chaotic, capricious and whimsical—was friend, lover, mother and sister. She was time and eternity. She was Saraswati, Lakshmi, Parvati. Everyone else could cut her trees, suck her waters dry and spit on her buildings. But not Kanti, no—he cared for Kathmandu.

He mourned her imperfections, like a teenager would a wart, a pimple, a scar. And slowly, he came to accept them, too—for, his love came with no conditions. Despite having known the city for more than twenty-five years, Kanti still explored her like a man learning a new lover.

The arrow of time may be infinite but space is limited; time can stretch forward but space can only fold into itself. Finally there are only so many paths to take, and Kanti found himself repeating alleyways once too often. He had always recognized places but now he came to expect them. He had always known where he was but now he knew where he was going and how he was going to get there. He began seeing familiar faces. This disturbed him deeply and he lay awake many nights. Sometimes, he considered now-recognizable figures; at times he traced paths in his head. He wondered if he ought to move to Patan or Bhaktapur and start over. It wasn't that he didn't want to live in Kathmandu anymore but that he had become too comfortable. He feared lapsing into a routine, as happened with so many intimate relationships. Then he would be no better than anyone else and together they would be no better than ants, wandering aimlessly, bumping into each other and then going the opposite way.

It was on one of these sleepless nights that Kanti decided to take a walk. It was well past ten, his usual bedtime, when he ventured out of his house and into the moonlight. The neighbours, whose accusatory gazes Kanti avoided each time he passed them by, were all in their homes, in front of TVs and under warm covers. He walked quietly and slowly. He had hardly passed the giant peepal-bot that divided his ward from the next when a strange exhilaration came over him. Beneath the pale, jaundiced moon, the houses loomed tall, the walls stretched to infinity and even the asphalt roads shone with a dull glow. There were shadows everywhere, long, deep ones that seemed to reach out with tapering fingers when Kanti came near. Except for the occasional car horn and the roar of a passing motorcycle, the air was punctuated only with the staccato barking of dogs. And here, even in the heart of the city, Kanti heard the trill of crickets.

He wandered further, driven by a rush of adrenaline. He recognized streets, stop signs and storefronts but suddenly they were of a quality vastly different; in semi-darkness, he found new textures, colours and shapes. The lettering on billboards seemed to shimmer and blend into each other with every passing motorist. Corners were sharper, angles more acute and every nook and cranny looked like the entrance to an underground extension. Sounds floated in intermittently from across town and he heard snatches of hushed conversation, the monotone of the television and the stifled moans of couples in love. Once, he heard a solitary scream pierce the night sky like an arrow and wondered if someone was trapped in a nightmare he couldn't wake up from. Even the smells were different. No longer did the air reek of burning rubber on asphalt or the noxious fumes of a thousand vehicles. Instead, the air was heavy with earthy scents and dampness— like just before rain—and the sickly sweet scent of decay. To Kanti, this was all oddly satisfying.

And so nights became Kanti's refuge. He still took his daily walks but they were merely preparatory, a warm-up for what was to come. After his first nocturnal jaunt, he started rationing his time outdoors, staying out three hours at the most in darkness, and always setting forth after his parents had fallen asleep. On returning home from such excursions, it would take him at least another hour to calm his double-beating heart and fall asleep. The next day, Kanti would go to work with swollen eyes.

Gradually, he began waking up late, then still later, and, as if in a daze, even found himself taking the bus to work. He filed, copied, stamped and signatured fewer papers and lunchtime was often spent at his desk, slumped over and asleep. His co-workers, who already thought him strange, began to avoid him, even the women. His parents stopped asking him where he was off to, even when they would catch him on their way to the bathroom, going in or coming out at odd hours. But Kanti himself was happier than he had been in a long while. He was a child again, exploring his neighbourhood for the first time.

It was an early April night when Kanti came across something he had never seen before. Idling by a corner of the main road, turning to the Radisson hotel incline was a bus. Kanti was very familiar with the kinds of buses that plied Kathmandu's streets and this was not one of them. It was deep crimson in colour, slightly longer than the average public bus but shorter than the distended tourist buses. It bore no lettering, not even a logo, and was humming steadily with its headlights on. Kanti got closer and saw that the bus' number plate was black—clearly it was a public bus.

Inside he could spot silhouettes of people. Kanti wondered if Kathmandu's ill-fated night-bus service had restarted. On a whim, he slunk in through the bus' open doors. There was no conductor to collect the fare. A row of lights illuminated the passenger section of the bus but the driver was shrouded in darkness. Kanti took an empty seat and looked around. Up ahead, a middle-aged woman in a formal office skirt and red lipstick stared unblinkingly out of her window. To his right, on the seat across the aisle, was an older man, maybe fifty years old, in a cream daura-suruwal and a black bhadgaunle topi. His hands were folded across his lap and he was staring at them intently. Kanti turned, and directly behind him sat another man, closer to his age, sunglasses perched on top of his head, a white polo shirt open at the neck and a thick gold chain girdling a forest of dark chest hair; this man seemed to be staring at an imaginary point somewhere past Kanti.

There were others. But before Kanti could observe them, the lights went out and the bus started to move. He tried to keep track of the route but everything looked distorted from his window. He started to get uneasy, not knowing where he was headed, so he tried asking the passengers. No one seemed to hear him. He called out to the driver but there was no answer. He waited for a while, hoping that the bus would make a stop and he could get off. But it kept moving. Kanti willed himself to get up and approach the driver, when finally the bus came to a halt. Kanti hurriedly got off. No conductor came to collect the fare and the bus, after dropping him off, silently slunk into the darkness.

The bus had travelled for less than ten minutes and within

that radius, Kanti knew every square metre. And yet he found himself confused, directionless and, for the first time in his young life, lost. This wasn't simply a trick of the night; the territory was alien. The buildings were impossibly tall, reaching for the clouds. The signs couldn't be read; Kanti recognized the individual letters but when he tried to put them together as words, they made no sense. Robbed of a cartographer's instinct, and rudderless in this vast, inky darkness, Kanti began to panic. This was a kind of fear that he had never experienced before and it spread through his body like a fever.

Kanti forced himself to walk and soon he was running, frantic, looking this way and that for any sign of familiarity, a corner, a cold store, a paan-pasal, anything. But the streets were as unfamiliar as the topography of a far-off, hostile planet. There was no sound, not even of dogs or crickets, and the sky changed and fluctuated, turning dark and light intermittently. He thought he passed people but he recognized nobody.

A heavy weight seemed to descend on Kanti. He finally stopped, out of breath and panting. Up ahead was a set of old wooden doors, the kind you find at the mouths of Asan's narrow corridors that lead to homes and courtyards. The doors were slightly ajar and Kanti entered one, not knowing what else to do. Within was a long, dark foyer, illuminated at the far end by a lone hanging bulb. Ahead were stairs leading up, each step branded by the tell-tale crimson of paan stains. As if beckoned, Kanti walked up the stairs, one hand on the cold metal railing. He reached the second floor, and another corridor. This corridor, too, was long and dark, illuminated, once more, at the far end by a lone hanging bulb. Again ahead of him were stairs leading up, each step also branded by paan stains. A set of old wooden doors waited by the bulb. Kanti pushed them open, calling out into the darkness. He hoped to find a room or an office, but he emerged into the street instead, back to the place from where he had entered.

Kanti did not go back in. Ahead was a brightly lit store window, its fluorescent glow attracting moths and abnormally large flies. Kanti was gripped by a reflection on the glass. Where he expected to see his own unsmiling visage, Kanti saw only the back of his head. Himself, looking at himself in the glass, looking at himself on the glass. Kanti thought back absurdly to the Colin glass cleaner his mother used around the house. The bottle had a picture of a woman holding a bottle of Colin with a picture of a woman holding a bottle of Colin.

'*Thik cha, bhai?*' A man, seemingly both young and old, came up to Kanti.

'Where am I?' Kanti asked, startled.

'Kathmandu,' said the man, either an indulgent smile or an annoying smirk playing on his lips.

'No,' said Kanti. 'I know Kathmandu and this is not it.'

'Isn't that a little vain?' asked the man, this time definitely sardonic.

'What is?'

'To assume that a place is not what it is simply because you don't recognize it. Cities, too, have masks.'

'Is this Kathmandu's mask?'

'*Huna sakcha,* all I know is that right now, this is the face she is choosing to show us. *Suna.* Just listen.'

At first, Kanti heard nothing, but then, slowly, beginning somewhere deep underneath his feet, he sensed a long, continuous rumble. The air around him quickened as the rumble rose from the earth and shook the air. Everything around seemed to vibrate, and then, abruptly—a dead calm.

'A breath.' Kanti knew it. He had always known it.

The man turned to go but Kanti called after him. 'How do I get back to Lazimpat?'

'Where is that?' asked the young-old man.

'Home,' said Kanti. '*Ghar.*'

'You're already home,' came the cryptic reply.

Kanti called after him but the man was already dissolving into the darkness. When Kanti followed, he found no trace of him, even though the street stretched on, straight and unrelenting, and a strange brightness seemed to have touched the air.

Kanti continued to wander. At times walking, at times running. The initial fear he had felt dissipated as Kanti lost himself in the ways the buildings seemed to sway in a non-existent breeze, like trees. Temples larger than hills loomed in the distance, their giant pagoda roofs like spreading umbrellas. In front of him, in the distance, was the Dharahara, jutting out like a defiant finger and, to his right, two more Dharaharas, two more fingers. Kanti looked to his left and when he turned around, all of the Dharaharas were crumbling to the ground. The vista was endlessly shifting shape and there seemed to be no limit to its permutations.

Maybe this truly was the real Kathmandu, thought Kanti. Or perhaps it was Kathmandu as she would like to be. Or even Kathmandu's dream. Kanti liked that last one. He liked to think of himself as being in Kathmandu's dream, just like Kathmandu had invaded his dreams on so many nights.

Kanti felt as if he had left himself behind somewhere, back in the old, familiar Kathmandu. Here, in the city's dreams, he was just a seeing eye, with no personality, no individuality. He might as well have been a seamless part of the city, a stone waterspout, a broken-down railing, a Basantapur pati, a New Road brick.

And, just as suddenly, Kanti woke up. This wasn't a waking from sleep, for he had never gone to sleep. But Kanti knew from experience that one didn't have to be asleep to wake up. Just as one didn't have to be awake to go to sleep. He found himself standing in the middle of a street in Asan. The close familiarity of the space rushed in like a wave and Kanti almost retched while people jostled him and bikes screeched. There were dogs, birds, cats and cows and so, so many people crowding around like midges. It was day, the light was too bright and Kanti felt too tired to walk home. So he did something he had never done before. He took a taxi home.

Kanti wondered where he had been and if he had ever really been there at all. The impressions of that fugue were already fading and Kanti found it harder and harder to retain memory. Those infinite towers, those flashes of light and day, those endless vicissitudes, arrangement upon arrangement. Sitting in a chair in his room, the same room he had had for twenty-five years, the same chair he had had for ten years, he came to the realization that he hated them both. The sameness was chafing, the fit was too tight and he began to feel suffocated.

He grasped at the last fleeting recollection of the mutating vistas and found in them a kind of comfort he had never found in the still and the static.

In the coming days, Kanti discovered that his zeal for walking had ebbed. The sense of permeating calm he found in his daily sojourns gave way to a discomfort at every sight, every smell and every sound. More and more he confined himself to his room and, on especially quiet days, he stopped and listened hard, hoping to hear the city breathing. He knew now that the city slept and dreamed itself into being. He wondered just how many buildings, roads and hills were dream figments. He wondered the same about the residents of Kathmandu, the men, women and children who traversed the streets, blissful, while underneath the city roiled and rumbled. Often, Kanti threw open the windows of his room, whose rusty, corrugated hinges squeaked mightily the first few times, and stared out at the city, unblinking. The distant hills were the same—green-brown and undulating. The roofs of buildings were the same, each sporting the same matte black cylindrical water tanks. The roads were the same, corners marked by rats' nests of wires atop telephone poles. Nothing had changed—and yet nothing was the same.

The Smoker

And again,

She crosses her legs and then uncrosses them. Eyes glued to her book, fingers poised to turn the page, she does it again. As I sit watching her, she repeats the action, habitually and without a second thought. Her gaze never leaves the book and neither do her fingers but her legs, jean-clad and long, ending in bright red pumps, continue to cross and uncross. A few seconds between each cross and each uncross, each movement spaced just far enough apart as to not call attention to it. I try not to stare, but my throat is dry and it takes me a full two minutes to get up. My head repeats a familiar mantra—maya, maya, maya.

The 7 train rolls in, creaking like an old man, and the subway doors open with a hiss, but I'm concentrating on her, afraid to lose her for even a second. People stream out of the doors and for a moment she is lost in the tide. When they pass, she's gone. I try frantically to reach the train, jostling elbows and knocking knees, but she is already at the door of a subway car, boarding it. I push past more people but the doors close before I can slip inside. She stands in the middle of the car facing me, the book held up to her face, obscuring it. I can see her hair and it looks exactly like it did the first time I saw her—which seems like so long ago—full and vibrant like a mane. As the train starts to move, I knock on the glass, hoping to catch her attention, but not once does she look up. I run along the car yelling to her but she makes no movement. I catch a glimpse of the book and its cover. She's reading Cortázar's *Rayuela*.

Then,

First came the frustration, the constant stream of crumpled balls of paper, the incessant nagging in the back of my mind, the flood of curses that would fill my head each time I wrote something that didn't make sense. I sat at my desk, day after night, bathed in the eerie blue glow of the computer in a dark, dank and increasingly chaotic room. I typed a word, deleted it, wrote a sentence, deleted it, completed a page and deleted it. When it had been more than two months of living like this, I began to give up.

All this time I read voraciously, hoping to spark off an idea. I desperately read Cortázar, Borges, James, Kafka and O'Connor. I plowed through collections, reading Calvino's short stories over and over again, as if they concealed a secret history. I visited the New York public library, sitting at the same desk day after day until the regulars there started to identify me as one of their own. Each day, I got a smooth nod of a shaved head from the fellow at the corner table, reading his newspapers, a smile from the cute girl poring over volumes of Burton's *Arabian Nights*. I religiously bought each issue of *The New Yorker* and *The Paris Review*, each of these bourgeois magazines making a sizeable dent on my already dwindling bank account.

After six months of this, I stopped reading. I started work at a deli where I was the only non-Korean employee. The two girls who worked with me almost always retired to a corner of the store the moment they got in. There they would chatter, becoming increasingly louder, leaving me to do all the work. If I ever called out to them, the answer was always shrill laughter and more chattering in Korean.

I did my part, working late, six days a week. There was always just enough money to cover rent and food and a little left over for a drink at a bar or a gram of ganja. Otherwise New York City was a big fat bloodsucker.

On the days I was working, I would collapse into a deep coma the minute I returned to my Astoria room. On my one day free, I tried to write the moment I woke up, but always gave up in about an hour or two. There was no internet to distract me, for I couldn't afford it. There was no television, for I couldn't afford that either. Not enough marijuana, no drugs, but sometimes there was alcohol.

Some mornings, if I didn't have to work, I would lay in my bed for hours, staring at the ceiling or out the window, sometimes trying to will an idea into existence, other times just pleading with whatever entity, whatever muse, to give me something, anything. But I always only received something so vague I couldn't even see its outline.

When I first met Maya, I had just been fired from the deli after being caught sneaking bottles of Snapple in my bag. She stood on the 7 train platform at Queensborough Plaza in a knee-length summer dress and bright red pumps. There was a slight breeze and when the wind gusted, she clutched the hem of her dress, afraid of a Monroe. Sitting on one of those hard wooden waiting benches with the raised furrows in between each seat, I saw her from behind but paid her little attention. Her red shoes caught my eyes but I only gave them a cursory glance. Pretty girls are as common as rats in New York.

We both got onto the 7 train at the same time and since there were no free seats, we stood next to each other, holding on to the cold metal pole. She flipped her hair and something that smelled fresh and like grapefruit wafted over me; I looked at her and she looked at me. Her eyes widened and she smiled.

'Pranaya,' she said. It was a statement, not a query.

I nodded.

'Pranaya from Sarah Lawrence,' she said again, affirmatively.

This time I shook my head no. I hadn't gone to Sarah Lawrence College, I had gone to Hunter in the city.

'Oh. My mistake, I thought you went to Sarah Lawrence,' she said flippantly. 'But you don't remember me?' She looked at me quizzically, her eyes moving back and forth across my face.

I blinked. Why was this girl talking to me? Her large brown eyes searched my face as I searched hers. Her face was framed by long, loose locks of hair, the darkest black, and there was a small mole on her neck, peeking out from beneath her curtain of hair. I was certain that I had never seen her before. I would've remembered her. She was striking. There was something in the jaunty tilt to her head and the set of her jaw, the line her compressed lips made. It was something odd, something out of place. I doubt anyone else would've called her beautiful, but when she talked, the left corner of her mouth creased a little in a half-smile, as if every word she spoke was some sort of inside joke. I felt mocked and, at once, intrigued. Her clavicles peeked out from beneath the straps of her dress and I couldn't stop staring at them, first the left, then the right—clearly defined bones that jutted from her body.

I said no, I didn't remember her.

She asked me if I was Nepali, if I was from Kathmandu and if I had gone to Rato Bangala School there. I nodded my affirmation to each of those questions, but still asked if she might've mistaken me for someone else.

'No, I know your face,' she said. 'You were just as thin then as you are now. And that hair, it used to be longer, but no, it's definitely you. I would've recognized you anywhere.' That half-smile was once again on the corner of her lips. 'We met in Kathmandu, at least twice.'

I didn't have to say anything.

'I'm Tara's friend,' she said, in Nepali.

I hadn't assumed she was Nepali. She didn't really look Nepali. Her nose was too aquiline, her complexion all wrong. I had pegged her for someone from the Middle East.

'I'm Maya and I'm a little offended that you don't remember me,' she said as she let go of the pole she was clutching. I apologized profusely, blaming my marijuana-addled college-brain for its lapse in memory.

'I'll let it go, but I am disappointed. I remember we had

some great conversations back then. We talked a lot. Weren't you working for a newspaper then?'

'Yes,' I said. I worked as a reporter for the *Nepali Times* before I made my way to New York for college.

We arrived at Jackson Heights, where I was getting off, and, as it turned out, so was she. We walked off the train and out of the station together. She did most of the talking, telling me what she remembered about me—the long ponytail I had back then, my aversion to gin, the ratty pair of Converse chucks I wore almost every single day. I wondered just how much she knew about me when I didn't remember her at all.

We sat down at an Indian restaurant, or rather she sat down and I followed. I didn't ask her where she was going and she didn't ask me either.

'I liked those stories you used to write,' she said, as we sat down. 'They were so angsty.' She smiled. She told me how she liked the one where a man gets addicted to the taste of ink from his pen and starts to spit out letters and words, the one where a woman, who turns out to be a prostitute, contemplates an unmarked box that has been entrusted to her, and the one where a man discovers that his city is alive and breathing. Over rice and chicken tikka, she described to me my stories. She knew each character as if they were people rather than caricatures on a page. She knew their backstory, their history, their family, lives, times and places. They were my stories, sure, but they were never this fleshed out in my head. My characters began and ended on the page. For Maya, they seemed to have actually lived.

I didn't say anything. Frankly, I was quite surprised that

someone had gleaned so much from some terribly amateurish stories I'd written years ago. I didn't remember sending them out to many friends but back then, emails had a habit of circulating. Here she was, this strange girl who kept brushing the hair out of her eyes, who knew everything about me and everything about my writing. Maybe she was a stalker, but then again, why would anyone stalk me?

She said she lived far into Brooklyn with two other girls. When I asked her what she did, she replied that she didn't do much of anything. She didn't go to school and she didn't have a job. When I asked her how she paid her rent, she looked a little surprised. 'Oh, I manage,' she said flippantly. 'This is New York. There are always ways.'

I had gone to college on a scholarship, I had barely a hundred dollars to my name, I had just lost my job, and the one thing that I had been relatively good at, I couldn't do anymore. And here she was—rich and pretty, parents probably paying her rent. And if not her parents, then some rich boyfriend. She had never worked a day in her life, her fingernails were perfectly shaped and clean, her palms smooth and unblemished. She came from privilege.

'Yes, this is New York,' I said.

'City of millions,' she said, leaning forward so that the ends of her hair nearly scraped the top of her curry.

'Who do you want to be today? Take your pick. Be one of the millions you see on the subway, one of the millions you pass at Grand Central. What possibility, huh? Each morning, you can step outside your apartment and decide to be a different person. Do you realize how exciting that is? How liberating?

Sometimes you never want to stop becoming another and another and another.' She was breathless now, her eyes haunted and staring. I half-heartedly tried to return her gaze but my eyes wandered off and up above a point behind her head. 'This isn't Nepal, this isn't Kathmandu, where everyone knows everyone else. Anonymity is amazing; as long as you're anonymous, everything is limitless. I put on a dress and I'm someone else. I put on jeans and I'm someone else. Don't you feel the need to step outside your skin sometimes?'

She leaned back, resting her elbows on the arms of her chair. Sitting across from her, hearing her talk with such abandon, such authority and ease, I could easily have fallen in love with her. I wondered if in the dark, dank attic of my memory, I had loved her in some other time. And maybe the fear of that love reciprocated, the fear of that intensity turned on me, like a magnifying glass on an ant, might just have destroyed me, maybe that was why I didn't remember her. Her gaze, her mannerisms, her voice, her hair, the way she crossed and uncrossed her legs unconsciously as she talked. I would never have forgotten her.

The rest of the meal passed almost in silence. She seemed finished, even though what she had said last didn't seem at all final. We made small talk, of some people I thought she might know but she didn't. I asked after Tara and Maya made some non-committal remark. I didn't push her to speak and the rest of our conversation consisted of even more banal generalities. She suddenly seemed preoccupied.

We parted ways outside the restaurant. She asked for my number but I gave her my address instead. I hadn't had a phone for some time now. But now that I was unemployed, I expected to be spending a lot more time at home. I watched her write down the address in a small brown Moleskine notebook, her handwriting precise and ordered, but her letters long and elegant. Before I could think of asking for her number, she'd already closed the notebook, placed it inside her handbag and walked off. I decided against following her and instead made my way to a little cafe down the street that my friends frequented. Avi and Onta were sitting at a table in the corner of the second floor, sipping tea. The three of us were able to come up with three Mayas that we had been friends with back in Kathmandu, but none of them matched the Maya I had just met.

It was dark by the time I made my way back home. There were no stars, only an inky blackness with wisps of dark grey. It isn't that easy to become someone different. It's not anything like changing your shirt. There are trials you go through, gauntlets you have to pass, there are scars and lots and lots of bruises, blue and purple. There are black eyes and beatdowns. There is lying on the floor after a hard night, unable to get into bed. The changes, when they come, are subtle. None as instantaneous as going grey overnight. Nothing as dramatic. Becoming is banal. It is what we do every day, in subtle ways we never notice. Becoming someone different is not about adopting a persona, it's about never admitting to yourself that you were ever anything other than this.

I don't know where Maya came from. Maybe, like Athena, she sprang from my head, fully formed. I tried to reconstruct her face in my head and I think I came away with mismatched eyes, fuller lips and a wider nose. I tried again and again; her eyes didn't seem to align, her hair was different and her mouth all wrong. I can recall her feet, her hands, the flatness of her stomach, the curve to her cheek and the flecks in her eyes, but when I try to put them together, when I try to describe her as concisely as I can, it never makes sense.

When I got home I tried to write and, for a second, I thought I had something. It was elusive, it came after two paragraphs of unending bile, but I could feel this newness, this germ of an idea coursing through my body. For a moment, who knows how long, my fingers moved faster and there were sentences. But this wasn't drivel, it wasn't drool from a dog's open jaw, it wasn't trash, it wasn't two rats gnawing at a piece of white, white bone. And then, just as easily, it was gone. I had managed two pages in a flurry. I stared at those words, turning them over and over in my head but not comprehending what they said. Instead of exhilaration, a vague unease settled in.

The shady employment agency by 72nd and Roosevelt was able to get me another job that very night. I was to start the night shift at another deli. It wasn't very different from my previous workplace minus the giggling girls. I shared the night shift, 9 p.m. to 4 a.m., with Freddy, a friendly Mexican who spoke little and worked a lot. The first time I met him, he shook my hand and then held his palm up, saying, 'Look. Six fingers.'

He did it to everyone he met. His extra finger, jutting out

of the left side of the thumb, was the first thing he ever mentioned. On slow nights, I would try to get Freddy to talk to me. One night, he took me into his confidence. Speaking English slowly and with difficulty he tried to explain to me his predicament. In his youth in Mexico, Freddy had been a drunk and a wastrel, a loafer, a 'tyape'. He had managed to get married to a young Filipina, a girl he had gotten pregnant. When his drinking got worse, she left him and came to America, taking Freddy's young daughter. Freddy's next drinking binge lasted five years, during which he lost touch with everyone he cared about—his wife, his family and his daughter. After the five years, he came to his senses, quit drinking and embarked on a quest to find his wife and daughter in America's vast expanse. Through a source he heard that his wife was in Washington, so he managed to get to Seattle, Washington, working his way up. Once there, he found out that his wife was in the other Washington—DC that is. But while in Seattle, he happened to catch a Nickelodeon show, *iCarly*, starring a Hispanic teenager.

'She is my daughter,' he said to me squarely. Freddy was convinced that this young actress, who he caught on television pretty regularly now, was his daughter. I tried to explain to him how unlikely that was but he wouldn't listen to me. I told him we could probably look up the names of her parents on the internet but he wouldn't hear of it. It wasn't something that occurred to him.

'Her mother is very beautiful, that is why my daughter, she doesn't look like me,' he explained earnestly. I hadn't the heart to argue with Freddy. He knew that she was his daughter. It wasn't something that could be debated. He had seen her on television and he knew. Don't parents always know their children? Or maybe that's just mothers.

Despite our thinking to the contrary, we believe in things we know to be irrational all the time. We claim to desire explanations to everything but just look at how much we let slide. Who knows why the sky is blue? Lots of people. But lots of people don't, and they couldn't be bothered to give a damn. Take god, whose very existence is rooted in irrationality. If you can explain god's existence rationally, then you're not really talking about god.

So who was I to blame Freddy? Or take away his happiness at seeing his daughter on television every day? He believed it and maybe that's what made it true.

Maya knocked on my door but entered without waiting for a reply. I blinked back the early morning haze and looked up at her, taller than ever, her hair pulled back in a ponytail. She looked different, her face more defined, more angular. Maybe it was the ponytail but now she looked like a completely different person, and yet it was her.

'You sleep late,' said Maya. 'I knocked a few times but you didn't answer and the door was unlocked.' It wasn't an apology, just a statement, made with a small smile. 'Are you naked?'

I was in my boxers and felt a little awkward having her there while I scrambled to put on a T-shirt and pants.

'I brought you something to read,' she said, and took out a

plain blue hardcover from her bag. In simple black font it said THE SMOKER. There was no title page, no publisher, no author. I asked Maya what it was about. 'It has nothing to do with smoking,' she said glibly.

I thanked her and put it aside just as she asked if I wanted to go for a walk. I agreed and we spent two hours at Astoria Park. We sat on a bench and watched a game of football between a team of Dominicans and a team of Indians. Maya sat next to me on a bench by the side, her body angled towards me a little, her hands in her lap. This time Maya barely said anything. It was a different Maya from the voluble, vivacious Maya I had met before. This was pensive Maya, lost-in-thought Maya, dreaming Maya, head-in-the-clouds Maya. I asked her if she was alright and she said yes.

A bulky Dominican managed to steal the ball from a bulkier Indian. He dribbled the ball past two defenders and made a feint towards the goalkeeper. The goalkeeper went for the ball, the Dominican flipped it just out of the Indian's reach and slammed the ball neatly into the net. And, as if blindsided by a truck on Tuesday, I saw colours. This was an epiphany. I had an idea. I asked Maya for her notebook and scribbled down all that came to my head. It followed from what I had written a week earlier, my last tryst with this new germinating idea. If I had run all the way back to my apartment, it would've melted away, like so many wisps of smoke.

When I had finished writing down all I could, I tore out the page and placed it in my pocket. I noticed the page behind the one I had just torn out had my address on it. Only it was the wrong address, 2340, not 2430; 2430 was on the next street over.

'I know,' she said.

I asked her if she had gone to the wrong building first but she said, 'No, I came straight to yours.'

I persisted, how had she then known it was the wrong address?

'I don't know,' she dismissed the question with a toss of her head. 'Maybe I just remembered it right. If you have a good memory, you don't need any kind of help.'

Cryptic Maya. I let it go, even though a vague sense of unease, one familiar now, crept in slowly. But I was too excited about my idea to care. I outlined it for Maya.

'I'm glad you're getting back to writing now,' she said, resting a light hand on my shoulder. I looked at her eyes and they seemed more black than brown in the light. Even her hair looked redder than the jet black it had been the day that I met her.

Maya left for the subway after our walk, and when I got home, I felt hot and sick. My forehead was warm and I was sweating heavily. I had to sit down and take a breath. My legs were getting weak and my vision blurry. I lay in bed for what seemed like hours but must've only been minutes. Each time I closed my eyes, there was a sharp stabbing pain behind my right eye, like a needle being jabbed from the inside out.

I don't remember why I got out of bed or even why I started walking the streets in my condition. I think I was looking for a pay phone. In my delirium, the streets all started to mesh into one. When I was finally a little coherent, I realized that I had made my way back to the park from earlier. I could make out two teams playing football in the dark, the sounds of impact strangely muted. I got closer and realized they were the same teams from before, the Dominicans and the Indians. It was a strange match, no calls, no grunts or yells, no smacks or smashes, just a silent version of the game I had watched earlier.

The air was doing me good and I felt better, the breeze cooling my feverish skin. I walked along the edge of the park, skirting the football players and their game. On the other side, I could see two people, a man and a woman, sitting on a park bench, conversing intently. The woman was talking, her hands moving expressively and the guy nodded occasionally, sometimes scribbling into a small notebook. It was me. I could tell. In the same way that I can tell the mirror is reflecting an accurate me and not some imposter, I could tell this man, on the bench, talking to this woman, was me.

It was me and it was Maya. She was talking, leading the conversation. Her gestures were pronounced, she was going into detail, she was interested and interesting. I watched myself talking to her, and all the while she talked, she crossed and uncrossed her legs.

I made my way back to my apartment, walking slowly. The fever was coming back with a vengeance. I thought about interrupting myself and Maya. I thought about dropping by to say hello to myself. I thought of saying hello to the second Maya. But they seemed busy; maybe it was important, what they were discussing. Eventually they got up and left, walking hand in hand towards the Broadway station.

I lay in bed, trying to sleep, all the while wondering if I was me. I knew myself instinctively, unconsciously. Don't we all? All I know is I recognized myself and I was another.

When I woke, I was still feverish and hot but my mind was buzzing with ideas. I searched for the scrap of paper from Maya's notebook and found it folded and creased deep in my jeans pocket. I sat down and started to write, all else fading into the buzz of the background. I had fifteen pages when I stopped. I dared not go back and read it. I wanted to finish it first, get it all down, and then I would go at it with a hacksaw.

I spent the day exhilarated. I went in to work despite not feeling well and Freddy sympathized. 'Sometimes in fever, I talk to myself,' he said, with his six-fingered hand on my shoulder.

The next day, Maya came to see me again. She brought me a pack of cigarettes.

'I don't smoke,' I said.

'You're a writer and you don't smoke?' she laughed. 'Don't tell me you don't drink either.' She threw the pack of Marlboros on the desk and took me out to lunch.

When we got back, she sat on the edge of my bed and started reading my worn copy of Cortázar's *Rayuela*. When I asked her what she wanted to do next, she said simply, 'Read.'

I sat at my computer and tried to continue writing. My fingers poised over the keyboard, I wished—a word, anything. Nothing. Nothing except the faint sound of breathing and the rustle of cotton as Maya moved and the rustle of paper as she turned a page. There was a drip in the bathroom sink. The fridge made a noise. The computer hummed. And inside my head, gears turned, turning nothing in return.

Light was streaming through my makeshift bedsheet curtain and it hit Maya on the bridge of her nose but she didn't seem to mind. Her eyes followed the words on the page and sometimes she would mouth them, a finger to her lips. Her hair held back with a long wooden pin, her lips were thinner, sterner. Her face less defined, bones absent where once they'd been absolutely pronounced. Maya but not Maya.

Maya, maya, maya, I repeated in my head. In Nepali, Maya is to love. In Sanskrit, Maya is this world, the veil of illusion, the maya jaal. Maya is the lie that is reality. At the moment of nirvana, there is moksh, freedom from maya. Who knows what this freedom entails? Only the Buddha. Maybe it's death, maybe it's suffering, maybe it's nothing at all. Or maybe all there is is an Idea.

I spent the next hour on the computer, playing video games while Maya read. She shifted from her position— sitting up to reading on her side. A little while later she was fast asleep, the book neatly dog-eared and shut beside her.

I covered her up with my blanket and lay down next to her, facing the ceiling. I was seized with an intense nausea, immediately and suddenly. There was a weakness pervasive to my body and, once again, I felt hot and sweaty. I wrapped an arm around my eyes and fell asleep to uneasy dreams.

On waking, the weakness and fever seemed to have subsided but the nausea had intensified. Maya was still asleep next to me, her hand wrapped around my waist. I reached over her without dislodging her hand and picked up my computer. The words came easy, as if floodgates had been let open. I wrote for hours and into the night. I filled up page after page, adding twenty more to the story. When I finally stopped, my right wrist made ominous cracking sounds as I rotated it. My fingers were cramped and hurt each time I tried to clench them. All this while Maya slept.

Maya's only signs of life were the steady rhythm of her heaving chest and the air escaping her parted lips in slow breathy exhalations. I reached over and brushed her hair away from where it had fallen into her mouth. I was afraid she'd wake up and find me touching her, I was afraid that she would get up and leave and never come back. Outside, the wind rattled the decaying old brown shutters, creeping in through the cracks around the windows. Even the air was hot and humid, the night breath of a rancid city. I shuddered in my bed. In the icteric yellow light of the street lamp, filtering through slats in the shutters, I made out the form of her body silhouetted against the sheer fabric of her cotton shirt. The garment, open at her neck, revealed the skin of her chest, the tops of her breasts, the hollow of her neck—and some insanity inside me said, ravage her, take her, fuck her.

In the faint half-light of the night, there were countless shadows, more nooks and crannies than I had ever encountered. The room felt more and more like a cell, cramped and claustrophobic, no room to pace, even the shutters looked like bars. I needed to leave the room.

Outside, I took a walk back to Astoria Park. It was empty, and except for an occasional car that sped by and the faint strains of Nina Simone from a nearby window, it was quiet. I looked for myself on the other side of the field but there was nothing except the rustling of leaves in the summer breeze. Maya or Moksh, I kept turning over in my head.

When I got back to my room, at least an hour later, she was gone. *Rayuela* was missing and a pack of Marlboros rested neatly on my desk.

In the days that followed, I smoked each and every last one of those Marlboros while reading and rereading my entire story obsessively. It seemed to be something fine and I was afraid it might be momentous. I edited and it was like reading someone else's work. I recognized very little of it, except for easy anecdotes. The idea, though, was something else, something completely alien to me and yet so familiar, so exhilaratingly good.

I chain-smoked cigarettes, editing all the time. At first they made me jittery and jumpy, I was always looking over my shoulder at every tiny noise, but eventually, they started to calm me down.

My story was about a coincidence of times. A fragment of time, a slice of time, an eternity of time, it was all the same, said the story. It was about forking time—time that chooses and the overlaps that occur. Time was a labyrinth and this story was a ball of string. Infinity was a reoccurrence, a constant reimaging of the same thing, the eternal return. It was all true, it was all like Borges said. My story was also a spiral. There was the choice of spinning this way or that way but, ultimately, it would return to the same place, only you might not recognize the place anymore. You will be you but you might not recognize yourself anymore.

Everything bleeds into everything else. Each barrier, each border is permeable, no matter what you might've been fooled into thinking. Words recall other words, places recall other places. Do we ever look at one place without thinking of another? My story is one mode of passage in a vast network of bleeding and breathing bodies. It is not something heavenly or divine but something base and primal. It is not a raising up of the senses but of a lowering down, back to our bodies and away from our minds. It is a feverish outpouring of sweat and blood, the commingling of bodies in the dust, panting and spent. The ejaculation of infinity, the endless orgasm. Do we know what the body can do?

And yet one little thing remains—the end. How to end it? All that has been said, all that hasn't been said, all depends on the end. Five pages, a thousand words, a paragraph and a half? I don't know what form it will take. But when it does, it will be complete. I will tell it, and in the telling transform it. Each time someone reads it, they will fashion it like clay, with the strength in their fingers and the will to create. This story will recall another story. Ad infinitum.

When I saw Maya for the last time, she brought a book bound together with a piece of felt. It was a tattered copy of Paul Auster's *City of Glass*, signed to me. On the opposite page was the fading address of an apartment in Brooklyn.

After handing me the book, she stood in front of me and took off her clothes. What was the form of her body then?

Lean, with breasts like pomegranates, or beautifully rounded, with hips and breasts that flared, I cannot seem to recall now even though it had seemed so vivid then. She kissed me slowly at first and we got into bed, not having said a word. She sat on me, her eyes heavy-lidded, and reached into her bag and pulled out a book. She read from Eliot's *Four Quartets* while she moved on top of me. The words came faster and faster, like stones from a slingshot, hard and fast and round. Her naked brown legs clutched at me like a vice while there were voices in my head, a million different voices, all androgynous. I stopped hearing Maya's voice, drowned out among the multitude. I caught snatches of ideas, of stories, of films and books and fables and plays. They were all there, floating in the nothing just beyond creation, just beyond orgasm. And then it was happening, the explosions and the fireworks and the unending stream of colour and voice, synesthesia. And there was infinity, a stream of consciousness that could be dipped into for any number of wellsprings, and it was all there, every single thing in the entire universe. Perfect, unending, blissful inspiration.

Maya collapsed. Her hair was wet and stringy, her body hot and sweaty, her breath against my neck warm and inviting. Her eyes were closed, *Four Quartets* dangling from her fingertips. By the time I wrapped her in a blanket and put her to bed, there was nothing left. There were no ideas anymore. I sat next to naked Maya and told her of my problems with memory. If our brains remember everything, why can we not recall them? Everything we ever need to know is all there, ripe for the taking, only everything is beyond walls ten feet high, impenetrable.

'We forget what a luxury forgetting is,' said Maya with her eyes still closed. 'Imagine what we'd do if we could never forget. If every waking moment you knew everything you had ever known before. How painful that would be, how crippling. Forgetting is not remembering's opposite, is it?' She opened her eyes and they were more brown than I had ever remembered them being. 'You forgot me,' she said.

Outside my building, on the stoop, we stood close together. She leaned in and held me close. I could've loved her, if she had just let me. I could've loved her forever. She said goodbye and left me with a kiss on the cheek and a squeeze of the palm. She had never left like this before, with this finality. I knew that she was really leaving.

I tried to finish my story later that night. When nothing seemed good enough, I read some of *The Smoker*. There was something familiar about it. Something that reminded me of me. As much as my current story was a product of mine, *The Smoker* could too just as easily have been mine. It was easy to see. When I read the words out loud, I could see myself.

Over the course of the next week, I tried to write, day after day, surviving only on cups of noodles and cigarettes. There was no ending. I walked a lot. I waited for Maya at the Queensborough train platform, at Astoria Park and at the restaurants we had been to. I didn't see her once. Not even someone who smelled like her.

I did run across Tara at the park one day. She was walking her Japanese Spitz on a long red leash and waved to me from the distance. We talked idly for a few minutes before I brought up Maya.

'Who?' she said, a little perplexed, tugging and coiling the leash around her hand.

And there it was. I could feel the world turning.

'I don't know any Maya.'

The world was turning and a fork had been chosen—a world without Maya.

I made my way down to Brooklyn later that week, following a Lefferts Boulevard address that I found in the Paul Auster book that she had given me. There was a faint smell of cardamom outside the olive green door and a large yellow stain on the wall beside it. I knocked and the door was opened by a young lady, pretty and petite. Her hair was pulled back in a severe ponytail and she was cradling an infant on her hip.

'Yes?' she said questioningly.

As politely as I could, I asked if Maya was around.

She gave a small laugh, and peered past me as if looking for someone else. 'Who put you up to this?' she said with a smile, still searching enthusiastically over my shoulder.

I told her I didn't know what she was talking about and repeated that I was just looking for Maya.

'You're looking for Maya?' she chuckled. 'Here, meet Maya.' And held out the girl child on her hip. Maya blinked back at me, barely a year old, and reached for my face.

I reached for her hand and let her hold my index finger as she giggled and gurgled. I apologized, stammered some sort of explanation, and was turning away when I ran into a man standing just behind me. He was about my height, wore glasses and had a receding hairline. Probably in his late twenties, he clutched at the shoulder straps of a small backpack.

'Hello.' He smiled at me. 'Were you just visiting?'

'He was looking for Maya,' said the woman from the doorway.

'Why?' asked the man, moving past me and into the apartment.

I explained that I was looking for my friend Maya whose address this was supposed to be.

'Are you Nepali?' the man asked when he had heard me out. When I nodded, he started to speak in Nepali. 'I don't know this Maya. I don't think there are really any other Nepali people in this area. I've been living here for close to five years now. The only Maya here is my daughter,' he said good-naturedly. 'Want to come in for a cup of tea?'

With tea in my hand, I tried to describe Maya, but the description I gave didn't seem accurate. I couldn't remember if her hair had been black or reddish brown the last time I had seen her. The first time I met her she had seemed so much taller than me, but that last night, I remember our eyes being on the same level. Both husband and wife shook their head at the vague description I gave. I told them I assumed that they would at least know who she was since she had given me a book with their address in it, but the man assured me that he regularly sold his books to thrift shops and used bookstores.

Halfway through the tea, the man introduced himself, 'What's your name, by the way? I'm Pranaya.'

I answered that my name, too, was Pranaya. At first he didn't believe me. His wife thought that I was still joking, that one of their friends had put me up to this. Then she thought that I was a distant relative come to visit her and this was my big joke. I had to show them my ID before they finally believed me.

When reason fails you, you have to believe in something. There is only so much reason can do for you. It can draw causes and effects and it labels the irrational as coincidences or anomalies. This man Pranaya had the same name as me, but I had gone to Rato Bangala School while he had gone to St Xavier's. And instead of going to Hunter in the city, he had gone to Sarah Lawrence College in Westchester, just like Maya had asked me so long ago. Pranaya now worked as a stringer for the *Associated Press*, writing short stories on the side. He'd been published a number of times.

I liked his life more than my own. Was he a different me or a future me? Were we ever the same and then separated during some traumatic incident like multiple personalities? Was I his doppelganger or was he mine? Was this what it was like to go insane?

On the way home from Brooklyn, I waited at Queensborough Plaza. I sat on one of the benches at the end of the platform, my hands deep in my pockets. There was a hum of voices, a few speaking Spanish, a few Hindi, and a steady low roar of machinery and cars from the streets below.

There would be no end to my story. Maybe that was the way it was supposed to be. Maybe that's how Maya would've liked it. After all, no story ever ends. There is always the after, what happens after the happily-ever-after, after the credits have rolled and the lights come on. I think that when you read a book, you reread every book you've ever read. In the endless repository that is your brain, each new word you read is born from the bed of every word you've ever read. Maybe Jung was right, maybe we do all draw from the same reservoir, but while some of us have water spouts, others still use divining rods. Just like each place recalls another place, each idea recalls another idea.

How do I find Maya in this infinite city? Its towers reach for the stars and its trains tunnel feet underground, shuttling forth millions along rat-infested tracks. This anonymous city is heartless. Like the angler fish's luminous bulb masks its hideous teeth and monstrous appetite, New York's grey steel and cold concrete hide underneath the bosoms of beautiful billboard models and a million pretty Manhattan lights. Just one among millions.

Down in the street, a car screeched and a horn blared. A man walked by in front of me, plugged into his earphones, bouncing his head to the beat. From the other end of the platform there was shrill laughter and a burst of loud Spanish. There was a woman sitting on another bench to the left of me. She was leaning back, a book in her hands, reading intensely. As she read, she crossed and uncrossed her long jean-clad legs, her pumps bright red.

Dashain

Later, from among the labyrinthine reaches of his mind, as if navigating swiftly through the gallis of Asan, Rabi would pluck one single image from that day. This image, although fleeting and trivial, seemed, to him, most significant. Lying in bed that night, muscles throbbing from the day's exertions, Rabi held that sight tight, as if it was the only one that made sense from amidst a sea of meaninglessness. He squeezed his eyes shut, wishing for sleep, and thought only of row after row of tiny goosebumps on an outstretched arm.

Rabi had woken up that morning to a strange emptiness in the pit of his stomach. It wasn't that he was hungry; in fact, the thought of food made him a little nauseous. He wasn't sick either, for everywhere else he felt fine. No headache, no stomach ache, no fever, just the feeling as if his stomach had been hollowed out in the night and everything removed. Gingerly, he made his way to the kitchen where preparations were fast underway for the day's Dashain party. On the dining table the fine dinnerware was out—gleaming ceramic plates, polished steel forks and spoons and clear glass dessert bowls. The house was filled with the smell of frying moong. Rabi stepped outside.

In the front yard, Tirtha, Rabi's father, was sitting on a stool, polishing a khukuri the length of his arm. Its blade gleamed wickedly in the morning light and Tirtha stroked its edge lovingly with a smaller sharpening knife. Rabi's two cousins, both slightly younger than him, were watching Tirtha with rapt attention. Next to Tirtha, a waist-tall goat watched balefully with wide eyes, shaking its floppy ears occasionally to dislodge flies. It chewed mechanically and bleated softly from time to time.

Rabi watched as if hypnotized. There was something dangerously alluring about the weapon, its hilt strong and wide, its blade weighted on one side and razor sharp on the other. Rabi had held the khukuri only once before and that too during his bratabandha. He had been fourteen then and the knife had felt like something alien in his hands. It was heavy and seemed to throb with a life of its own. He had even been a little scared of it. Now all he wanted to do was run his finger down its edge hard enough to draw blood.

'So when is Mukul getting here, huh?' Tirtha yelled through the door frame to his wife, who was currently dabbing the rice cooker with butter.

'I don't know, he should be here soon. He said he wanted to watch the maar,' yelled back Sunita.

'That lutey is going to watch the death blow? I'm afraid he might faint,' said Tirtha to the boys watching him. 'Here.' He blew on the blade, wiped it off with the sleeve of his shirt and handed it to Rabi, who eagerly grasped it and began hefting it in his hands.

'What do you think?' asked Tirtha, watching Rabi intently.

'I think I could kill something with this,' said Rabi, awed by the knife.

'Heh,' Tirtha dismissed Rabi with a snicker. 'Maybe start with a chicken, they're smaller and easier. Today you can watch your father kill this khasi.' He affectionately patted the horned head next to him while the animal, oblivious to its impending fate, continued to chew quietly.

'Mukul uncle is coming today?' asked Rabi, suddenly remembering.

'Something wrong with your ears, chora? Didn't I just ask your mother when Mukul was going to get here? Of course he's coming and he's bringing that murkha wife of his and his chori too.'

Rabi's ears perked up. Mukul uncle was bringing his daughter and Rabi had had a crush on Varsha ever since he was twelve, when he had first started noticing the curves of her calves and the tautness of her stomach. Mukul and Tirtha had been good friends for years now and periodically took their families on outings. Varsha and Rabi, both being only children, were always stuck together. But Varsha was seventeen now, a year older than him, and rarely spoke to him at parties and such. It wasn't that she disliked Rabi, more that she had gotten accustomed to his ways. His quiet gaze, soft voice and shy manner didn't stir in her the kind of longing she felt for the bombastic guys at schools. Loud and obnoxious, they repelled her with their manner, and yet she was strangely attracted to them. They had long hair, early beards and rode flashy motorbikes with gaudy stickers on the side. Rabi, on the other hand, could barely ride a bicycle and the few errant strands on his chin were more a tease than an actual statement.

'Let me kill the goat,' Rabi blurted out suddenly, his mind replaying Varsha's long lashes.

'What?' Tirtha asked incredulously. 'Have you gone insane?' He laughed.

'No, I'm serious, bua. Let me do it. I killed a chicken at my mamaghar in Bardiya when I was fourteen.'

'When did you do that?'

'In Bardiya, when mom and I went to visit her family. Everyone told me I had to.'

'A chicken and a goat are two very different animals. Do you see how big this khasi is?' Tirtha's large hands rested lightly on the goat's head, fingering its horns. 'Do you really think that you could cut off this head in one clean blow?'

'Yes,' said Rabi immediately. He thought of how wide Varsha's eyes would get, how she might shake inwardly with attraction and how he might make her legs buckle. He would hold the khukuri aloft, blood dripping from its edge, and she would know he was more of a man than any of those guys she liked. 'I can do it. I know I can. Just give me a chance,' pleaded Rabi, his eyes shining.

Tirtha studied his son carefully. The boy was only sixteen but he was already taller than Tirtha. Sure, he was a little on the skinny side, but at least there were muscles and not fat. Rabi wasn't too interested in sports and didn't play football, to Tirtha's extreme disappointment. He liked books and studies and never seemed to go out much with his friends. Frankly, Tirtha was beginning to worry about the boy. 'Go out, get drunk, meet women, have a good time,' Tirtha wanted to yell at Rabi sometimes. Not this staying at home, reading books business. He privately blamed his wife for Rabi's tendencies. She smothered him too much. If he went out sometimes, she would hound him with questions on where he was going, who he was going with and when he would be back. If he came back after dark, she would be waiting at the door and would pounce on him like a cat, sniffing his clothes and hair for cigarette smoke and his breath for alcohol. Tirtha was often disappointed when she didn't find any.

Now the boy wanted to kill a goat. This was the first time that Rabi was showing interest in anything remotely manly. He was sixteen, in Class 10, and didn't even have a girlfriend. Although Tirtha would never admit it to himself, he fleetingly wondered if his son was gay. But here was a chance, a perfect chance for the boy to learn, to become a man like his father. Once the boy felt the warm blood, the ebb and flow of life and the goat's violently thrashing body, maybe that would transform him from a lutey into a man.

'Okay,' he said.

'Really?' It was Rabi's turn to be incredulous. Now that Tirtha had agreed, Rabi felt a little nervous. He had never swung a khukuri except to behead that chicken and that, too, he had done with his eyes closed. He had felt the spray of blood on his face and T-shirt and his hands felt warm to the touch even an hour later. But a chicken was small and inoffensive. A goat was a different thing altogether. They had ears like a spaniel's and eyes that seemed to search your soul.

'Yes, yes. Unless you've changed your mind. If you don't want to, I'm sure one of these other boys would be more than happy to try,' Tirtha played Rabi off of his cousins. The two boys, Sanjay and Bijay, leapt at the chance, talking over each other, trying to win Tirtha's favour so they might get a chance to lop off the goat's head.

'No, no, I'll do it. I want to,' said Rabi.

'Good for you, chora. It's about time,' said Tirtha with more than a hint of pride. 'Now, remember, you have to behead the goat in a single blow. If not, bad luck for us and especially during Dashain.'

'I can do it, bua,' Rabi said thoughtfully. In fact, he wasn't at all sure if he would be able to do it. Taking the khukuri back from his father, Rabi left the yard. Locked in his room, he stripped down to his underwear and stood in front of the mirror. He surveyed his body. He wasn't particularly strong but at least he wasn't fat or too skinny. He was of average weight, and tall for his age. Whenever he played basketball, the only sport he ever really enjoyed, he directed the ball easily with his long arms, grounded firmly by his equally long legs. He flexed in the mirror and noted approvingly the taut muscles in his biceps, shoulders and chest. He clenched his stomach and watched the outline of his abdomen emerge in a firm six-pack. He brandished the khukuri in his right hand, holding it tight, and swung it through the air. He held it with both hands, standing in front of an imaginary goat and brought it down hard, the air whistling as the knife cut through it. He practised again and again, bringing down the knife, his eyes shining at the prospect of adoration.

Mukul arrived soon with his wife and Varsha in tow. The goat was already tied to the stake and Tirtha, already positioned towards the goat's rear, yelled at Rabi to make his appearance.

Half of the guests for the day's party had arrived and numerous uncles, aunts and cousins stood around, more than half hoping, discreetly, for a travesty. It was now mid-morning and the sun was high. Although it was bright and sunny, there was a chill in the air and those who were underdressed wrapped their arms around themselves to gain some respite from the weather.

When Rabi appeared a cheer went up. His cousins were already mocking him, partly out of respect and partly out of spite. None of them had ever beheaded anything. Varsha stood to one side, her eyes distracted. She was wearing a bright yellow kurta with matching shoes, maybe a little showy for this Dashain gathering. No matter. Varsha liked to look good.

Rabi was wearing an undershirt and shorts. Mukul, standing by Varsha's side, followed her gaze and found himself approving of the boy who was almost like a son to him. Tirtha and Mukul had each watched the other's children grow up and privately, under the heady influence of a few pegs of Johnnie Walker Black Label, the two had discussed, quite often, the betrothal of their children.

Rabi sauntered towards the goat slowly and methodically, placing one sure step in front of the other. He knew now what the hollow feeling in his stomach was. It was fear. Rabi was shivering inwardly while outwardly, his body felt no cold. The khukuri was heavy in his hands and with each step, he drew closer to faltering. But he saw his father, crouched behind the goat, holding its legs tight, while in front stood Mukul uncle holding taut a rope tied around the goat's neck. Rabi looked for Varsha and, for a millisecond, he thought he saw a smile on her lips but then it was gone. He positioned himself at the head of the goat, took a deep breath and held it.

The goat, sensing something primordially, began to thrash about. Mukul splashed some water out of a karuwa on its head and the goat shivered involuntarily to dislodge the water from its eyes. Tirtha held fast to its back legs while Mukul pulled the rope tighter. Rabi planted his feet apart, digging them into the ground. He raised the khukuri high above his head, closed his eyes and said a silent prayer. Eyes open, he gauged the direction, the distance and in the split of a second, air whistling around the knife, with all the strength he could muster, from every yearning cell in every stretching muscle, he brought the khukuri down on the goat's neck.

There was a sharp, surprised bleat and a solid thunk as the knife bit deep into the goat's neck. Rabi felt the blade's passage through air, then into fur, flesh and bone. And there it stuck. The goat bleated terribly, a strange garbled cry that seemed to emanate not from its mouth but directly from its throat. There was a splatter of blood and Rabi felt the droplets warm against his neck and scalding on his face. He tried to pry out the khukuri but it was stuck fast, hard into the bone. The goat thrashed about, bleeding weakly out the side of the wound where the khukuri was stuck. As Rabi struggled with the blade, without even wanting to look, he saw Varsha, one hand outstretched, as if in protest, and the other covering her mouth. Rabi saw her arm, close as it was to him, and, while struggling mightily with the khukuri, saw clearly and closely, as if magnified, the goosebumps there. Her otherwise smooth arm, cleaned recently of all offending hair, was covered in row after row of tiny little bumps, like a symptom of some exotic disease. Rabi only had a moment to acknowledge it before he was jerked out of his reverie by Tirtha.

'Kill it, saley. Kill the bloody thing,' he yelled furiously, still hanging on to the goat's wild back legs.

Rabi summoned what little strength he had left and jerked the khukuri out of the goat's neck. He raised it again and brought it down once more. But the strength had gone out of his arms and the initial rush the adrenaline had fed had now turned his arms weak and ineffectual. The khukuri again bit into the goat's neck but hardly went further than the initial wound. He raised it and brought it down again, a sickeningly loud crunch as the goat's neck crumpled under the force of the blow, not cut but shattered. Its neck was dangling, half-severed from its body. Its eyes were glassy and red-rimmed and its tongue protruded from its mouth. Again, he raised the khukuri and brought it down. Again and again and again, until he wasn't cutting so much as bludgeoning the goat's lifeless body.

By the end Rabi was kneeling on the ground in a pool of blood. The goat's head was off to one side, leaking blood that Tirtha was collecting in a bowl. The body was still twitching, its legs stiff and stretched out, spraying blood in irregular spurts. The boy knelt in front of the goat, bloody teardrops on his eyelashes and silent blood droplets dripping from his sweaty, lanky hair. His chest was heaving and his breath came in gasps.

Slowly, Rabi stood up. The khukuri fell from his hands in a clatter. Tirtha stepped forward but Rabi waved him aside with a casual flip of his head. He trudged into the house barefoot, as if catatonic, leaving bloody footprints on the cement floor. He walked quietly into the shower where he washed himself for close to two hours, alternating between extreme hot and extreme cold.

When he came out to lunch, the goat had been skinned, cut and cooked and a heady aroma was wafting through the house. Conversation petered out when Rabi appeared. His cousins made jokes but Rabi heard nothing. His father half-heartedly clapped him on the shoulder, all the while thinking of the bad luck his son had invited with his merciless hacking. Mukul, who had changed into one of Tirtha's shirts, seemed happier than most and beamed at Rabi from afar, his arm protectively around his daughter.

Varsha did not look up at Rabi. She had felt something indefinable watching Rabi and the goat. It was a mixture of disgust and pity and she couldn't quite discern which she felt more. She had known Rabi ever since they were children and the relationship they had built over the years had become more fraternal than anything. She felt a deep love for Rabi, the kind that develops when you know someone for a long time, skeletons and all. Rabi disgusted her a little but she also couldn't help but feel sorry for his disastrous attempt at leapfrogging into manhood.

Rabi didn't speak or smile much. He sat down to lunch and ate heartily of the animal he had just slaughtered. Normally, he would've complained about the goat meat's animal odour, he would've commented on its gaminess. This time he simply took mouthful after mouthful, not really tasting the meat. He imagined vigour and vitality coursing through the flesh he was devouring. But despite how much he ate, he felt no life in himself.

Afterwards, he locked himself in his room and refused to come out. He watched through his window as all the guests left. He watched Varsha as she bent to pass under the narrow foot gate and felt no desire. The hollowness that had begun in his abdomen seemed to have permeated through his skin into his organs and deep into his being. He watched the minute hand on his wall clock as it made two complete circles, taking comfort in its excruciatingly slow but regular rhythm. Then he wished for sleep.

Our Ruin

As the record spun, I twirled a lock of Tara's hair around my finger, mimicking the movement, keeping time with the scratches and odd clicks the old, russet gramophone made. She lay with her head on my lap, legs hanging off of the side of the bed. Prasit sat on the floor, cross-legged, and resting back on his hands, palms flat on the carpet. As Dylan's nasal cadence filled the spaces between us, his guitar like a drum, we didn't speak for the longest time. The vinyl kept spinning and we sat in silence. Were we thirteen or fourteen? I don't even remember. I have trouble with time, less so with place and space. There's that record spinning and Bob Dylan in the air.

We were in Prasit's room, neat and ordered, everything in its proper place. Tara and I were on the bed and Prasit on the floor. I remember how she looked then, so young, her face smooth and unblemished, except for that one little dark spot on her left cheek. Her hair was full and smelled of oranges, sweet and tangy. Prasit was a nerdy little kid then. He wore his jeans high and his glasses were always coming loose. He'd push them up with the middle finger of his right hand, a nervous unconscious move.

We'd been hearing about Bob Dylan for a while now. Our

fathers and uncles tried to claim him for their own. They'd grown up in the sixties and they talked as if they'd lived with Dylan, singing 'Blowin' in the Wind' in hippie circles. It was only a matter of time before Prasit unearthed a Dylan record among his father's old Led Zeppelin albums, ones he'd collected during his days running a guesthouse on Freak Street in the early 1980s.

So, that day, a Monday or a Wednesday, all three of us were wearing school uniforms, ugly plain white shirts with blue pants or skirts. Tara's, and really all of the girls', loose shirts offered glimpses of skin from between the buttons and I often stole a look, only to always feel guilty later.

Prasit played the song. The record was *The Freewheelin' Bob Dylan* and the first scratchy song that spilled from that rusted funnel was 'Girl from the North Country', the album's second track. I don't know why we skipped 'Blowin' in the Wind', the first track, but I'm glad it was 'Girl from the North Country' we heard first. We said nothing when the song ended but Prasit moved the needle back and replayed it. We listened to the emptiness that seemed to run through the entire song, those gaps in between words that seemed to shine. It was spare, and everything we weren't used to. Back then we listened to Nirvana, Guns N' Roses, Metallica, anything loud, but right then, listening to Dylan, I was slightly afraid. I didn't know what to make of this. I had never heard such eloquence. Right then it felt like all I had been listening to previously was just noise.

Prasit kept replaying the song and, after maybe the fifth time, he finally stopped. Tara still rested on my lap, the back of her head digging into my thighs. Her eyes were closed and a slight smile played on her lips. I brushed a few errant strands away from her face. We had a conversation then. I don't think we talked about the song. I don't think we talked about anything important because our minds were still occupied with what we had just heard. And, in my memory, that was the first time I actually felt a connection with them. Before that we were just friends. We hung out a lot at school and at Prasit's and Tara's homes after school, but it was then that I actually felt like we were something more. Right then they stopped being just my friends. In that space of time when the song was still reverberating off of Prasit's egg-white walls, I finally realized that, in some strange teenage way, I loved them both. I had known them ever since I started school. Prasit and I had become friends in Class 2 and Tara became friends with us in Class 4. But then, right there in that room, I loved them both with a passion that frightened me. This was a passion I reserved for my mother, my brother. Not my friends.

Our last Class 10 exam was on a Wednesday. All three of us had optional mathematics as our final exams and, when the bell rang, we passed forward our papers like good kids, packed up our pens, pencils and calculators quietly, walked out of the classrooms in single file and then, once outside, we erupted. Pages torn from books rained down on us from above; there were screams, actual screams, of joy and liberation. Books and papers were shredded, kids hugged each other with fierceness and there was pandemonium. I ran outside and waited for Prasit and Tara. The moment they showed up, we took off.

Prasit's Hero Honda CBZ easily supported the three of us, not that any of us weighed more than sixty kilograms each. Prasit didn't even have a license then, but we didn't care. Our school exams were over, and if we got caught, we would beg forgiveness from the traffic police.

I squeezed in behind Tara on the CBZ and held her waist. Prasit sped off, manoeuvring the machine down narrow alleyways in order to bypass the traffic cops patrolling Kathmandu's major thoroughfares. From Lagankhel we turned into a narrow stone-topped alley with high brick walls on each side. Prasit didn't slow down; he manoeuvered the motorcycle as if it were part of his own body, moving with the ease of one well-practiced. Tara let out little screams from time to time, when her bare knees would almost brush against the hard walls. Luckily we soon emerged onto a bigger path. From there we rode on to Satdobato, where we took a highway leading south.

Prasit knew exactly where he was going. I had a vague idea too, but Tara complained constantly. She wanted a drink, she wanted a smoke, she was uncomfortable, where were we going, what were we going to do later tonight. Eventually, when both of us didn't answer, she stopped talking.

Prasit stopped the bike abruptly in front of a dilapidated gate. There were gaps in the brick walls leading from the gate and around the entire property. Well off of the main highway, around ten minutes down a narrow dirt path, just big enough for a car, the gate lay hidden from view by a mass of undergrowth. There was a small beaten path leading straight through the brush. Trees stood like massive Roman columns among the dense shrub. Two minutes from the gate, we came upon what Prasit wanted us to see. A neat little brick structure stood among the trees.

'This is Boris' house,' said Prasit, without fanfare.

'Who's Boris?' asked Tara meekly. I could tell she was scared. I didn't blame her. The place was eerie, too silent.

'Boris was the first tourism guy in Nepal,' Prasit said. 'I think he was European, German or something. Anyway, this was his house. He lived here with his wife but after he died, vagrants and thieves harassed his wife so much that she just abandoned the house. I think she never really got around to selling it either.'

It was a strange house, completely devoid of any kind of paint. The doors and windows were missing from their frames. They looked like empty eye sockets. Strange graffiti adorned the walls, both inside and outside. We peered in through the windows and saw a shoe, underwear, condoms, hypodermic needles and empty liquor bottles.

Prasit and I wanted to go inside but Tara refused. It was an interesting house, a little creepy maybe, but it had allure. I wanted to explore it, walk its empty hallways and rooms. So Prasit kept Tara company while I went inside.

There was broken glass everywhere. Bricks and concrete lay in chunks all over the floor, victims of senseless assault. The rooms on the ground floor reeked of urine and shit and the walls were plastered with a strange material that seemed to be congealing like dried blood. The wooden staircase that led to the second floor had been cruelly decimated, leaving only two pieces of wood, like broken collarbones, gaping from the wide staircase hole. I jumped up, grabbed the ends, and pulled myself up with ease.

Upstairs was cleaner in some ways. There were a few condoms and drug paraphernalia but less urine and feces. A rusty metal ladder led to the rooftop and, thankfully, this hadn't been destroyed. I climbed up gingerly, careful not to cut or scrape myself.

The rooftop was a square open space, lined with leaves from the trees surrounding it. It was a beautiful space, with soft light filtering through the canopy of trees. There was little refuse up here, probably because the addicts who frequented this place were too lazy, or high, to climb up. Like an oasis, the place lay shrouded amidst the waste. It was the perfect place for us. I walked to the edge and called out to Tara and Prasit.

It was difficult getting Tara up, but we managed. Prasit and I both grabbed one of her arms and hauled her up bodily. She complained that her arms had been jerked out of their sockets. We sat on a bed of leaves, making sure there was no trash nearby. Prasit produced a small bottle of Red Label and we drank slowly, taking swigs straight from the bottle. Tara pulled out her portable iPod speakers and we listened to Sufjan Stevens in shady light. 'Jacksonville' carried in the silence of the surrounding forest. It echoed from tree to tree and I imagined the song as something real, something solid, bouncing along, reverberating in a space that it had never occupied before.

'What's going to happen to us now?' It was a question I had longed to ask for so long but never had the courage to articulate. It was Tara who finally asked what I couldn't.

'Nothing,' Prasit replied.

'But where do we go? Have you even thought of what you're going to do now? Are you going to do Plus Two or A Levels or what?' I asked him.

'Well, I'm doing whatever you guys are doing,' said Tara dreamily. 'I don't know what I want to do with my life. I'm fifteen, I've just finished my SLC, I really don't care right now.'

'Yeah, we go together, right?' Prasit said, looking at me.

'Yeah,' I answered, looking right back.

Age snuck up on us like something malicious in the dark. It came up from behind and pounced when we weren't looking. Suddenly I looked around and realized just how much older we all were. In Class 12, Prasit and I had only just turned eighteen while Tara was still seventeen. Prasit had a beard now, a small outcropping of hair on his chin, defiant against the smoothness of his boyish cheeks. Tara had long hair and was still so beautiful. Only I felt unchanged and, before long, I felt like I didn't belong with them.

It happened so gradually I barely noticed. On their own these changes seemed like minor things, but seen from afar, the little things seemed to meld into something bigger, forming a picture I didn't particularly like. Prasit wore contacts now, grey ones that made his eyes look like slits. His hair was long and he always tied it back in a ponytail. He'd bought a new motorcycle, a Royal Enfield, one that sounded like a shotgun each time he started it up. He was smart and silent.

Tara was still lovely, with dark, sharp eyes and a mischievous grin. To me she just seemed like a bigger version of the girl I'd always known. Tara's changes happened inwardly. She'd always been silent and shy but now she was confident, even aggressive. She talked constantly, rambled mostly. When she talked, I felt like she was overcompensating for something.

Whenever we hung out with other people, I felt insignificant and invisible. No one talked to me; no one seemed to be interested in what I had to say. Tara was the funny extrovert while Prasit was the smart introvert. That left nothing for me. I had no role to fulfill and nothing else to offer. But then, whenever it was just the three of us, it felt like nothing was wrong. Tara was still Tara and Prasit was always Prasit, both my closest friends.

Of course, others began to intrude on our snug little threesome. Our circle of friends had grown. Sometimes, at home, I would put on some music and close my eyes. I would try and conjure up pleasing images, a puppy, ice cream, Angelina Jolie, mint cookies, and almost always Prasit and Tara. And we'd be listening to music. Most often it was Bob Dylan, but then there was also Pink Floyd in Tara's room, Led Zeppelin in Tara's living room, The Beatles in my room, Sufjan Stevens on the roof of Boris' house. I had also started listening to Nepali music, particularly Narayan Gopal, whose voice struck me as something torn and weary, an alcoholic's voice. I had tried making Prasit and Tara listen to him but they never seemed interested and it always felt like I was forcing it on them.

Despite all of our changes, we still managed to make it quite regularly to Boris' house. Every Saturday we'd meet outside Prasit's house. We'd buy some booze, cigarettes and ganja.

Sometimes there would be an extra person or two but we always managed to get there. Tara had a scooter now so it was a little easier. Prasit would lead and most of the times I would ride behind him, but if Tara was wearing a skirt, I'd sit behind her on her scooter, just to make sure that every guy who leered at her got a heavy stare-down.

We always climbed up to the roof, and we always hauled Tara up by her armpits. We never had an incident there. We never got too drunk or too stoned. Always enough to have interesting conversations but never so that we couldn't ride. A few times we had run-ins with the junkies who frequented the house. They were never there on Saturdays, which is why we picked that day. Usually, on weekday evenings, there would be some five or six people, shooting up, smoking, drinking, having sex.

The first time they saw us, they ignored us. This was on our third visit to the house. Before that we'd seen only traces of them. We didn't go into the house but just sat outside on the grass. Prasit and I built a fire and we drank quietly, talking amongst ourselves. Soon two of the junkies came over. They were haggard-looking, deep bags of skin hanging limply from under their eyes, skin white, dry and flaking, and their frames so thin and stiff, they looked like they would snap in a gale. They sat around our fire and talked to us. They stared for an uncomfortably long time at Tara and I found myself looking around for a rock, a stick, anything. But they did nothing, just talked to us about life, school, girlfriends and boyfriends. They asked us if we had any maal and we meekly said no. Eventually they asked us for some money. We forked over fifty rupees and that seemed like enough. A few minutes later they left.

That was the first time; the second time, they weren't so friendly. It was maybe a month or two after our first encounter. It was the three of us again and there were five of them inside the house. We saw them through one of the broken windows and decided to sit outside. We didn't build a fire this time, even though it was cold. We were smoking a joint, when two guys and a girl came out towards us. Past them, I could see another guy and girl wrestling about on the ground, kissing madly.

'*Phuchheharu lai*, no entry,' one of the guys said. He hadn't been here the last time. He was taller than the rest of them, bald, and didn't look as pasty or as weak as the others. But his arms were the same, dotted with little points of dried blood and blue with bruised veins. 'It's not safe,' the other guy said. He was familiar, shorter and smaller, with bleached dirty blond hair.

'We'll leave soon,' I said, trying not to look them straight in the eye.

The bald guy squatted on his haunches in front of us. He looked Tara straight in the eye, reached out a hand and brushed a lock of her hair away. Once again, I found myself frantically looking around for anything I could use to bludgeon this junkie to death, if it came to that.

I could tell Tara was scared. Her eyes were open wide but she wasn't saying anything. She was looking down at her legs, fiddling with the laces of her Converse. The bald guy still seemed very interested in her.

Abruptly, he stood up. 'Come here as often as you want,' he said, smirking evilly. 'Just as long as you bring her along,' he added over his shoulder as the three of them went back inside the house.

That little incident didn't deter us. School work stopped us from going after school but we almost always made it there on Saturdays. It became our own little ruin on Saturdays. We listened to all kinds of music on Tara's iPod speakers. I kept playing Nepali music, from Narayan Gopal to Jhilke and the Rockers and Nepathya, but it never seemed to click. Tara or Prasit would just go back to Pearl Jam or Bob Dylan after my song ended.

I even tried reading them Bhupi Sherchan once. Living in Kathmandu, going to a school that taught us in English, we had learned to speak English and think in English. We could barely remember how to count to eighty-seven in Nepali. But there I read Nepali poetry, and it felt like I had finally accomplished something real. But that too failed to stir something in them the way reading Walt Whitman did. Nevertheless we kept our conversations.

By the end of our A Levels, we'd grown considerably apart. Prasit had a girlfriend and Tara had an endless stream of suitors. Every day she'd relate to me a new tale of some poor sap who'd been unlucky enough to fall for her. She didn't go out for long with any of them, just flirted and led them on mercilessly.

I started going out with a girl named Rinchin. She was Tibetan, with a curtain of straight black hair that came down to her shoulders and bangs that made her look younger than she actually was. I don't know what she saw in me but it was she who first professed interest. I went along for the ride, unable to resist being drawn in.

The first time we missed our Saturday at Boris' place, none of us said anything. Prasit was spending time with his girlfriend, Tara was on a date with two of the guys who liked her and I was in my room, waiting for them to call. When it became obvious that they wouldn't, I went over to Rinchin's and we watched *Fight Club* together. She cringed when Edward Norton shot himself in the face, her body tight and warm against my side. I thought she loved me but I never knew what I felt for her. I told her I loved her but I doubt I ever meant it. What did I know of love anyway?

Rinchin was a lovely girl but also insanely jealous. She resented my close friendship with Tara and I believe she saw straight through me. She was a smart girl. Whenever we had fights, she would always bring up Tara. How I was obsessed with her, how I never talked about anything but what Tara did. Rinchin brought everything to the surface.

From the deep, well-hidden dregs of my soul, she drew out my feelings for Tara, placed them on the surface of a table and made me look at them, scrutinize them for what they were.

We missed another Saturday. The same reasons as the last time. The third Saturday, I called up Prasit and he agreed to come. Tara just couldn't make it. I didn't even think to ask Rinchin, even though I knew she would be angry when she found out I hadn't taken her along. It would just be Prasit and I on this trip. He picked me up on his Enfield and we made our way to Boris' house.

This time the shrubs seemed denser, the trees higher and broader, even the house itself was more dilapidated than before. An entire wall was missing, the bricks having been picked apart and stolen. With the wall missing, it looked like a garage, with the door up, and also like a gaping maw, the inside dark and frightful. We climbed up to our usual spot and we smoked a long joint, passing it back and forth for what seemed an eternity. The sun went down quickly, drenching the horizon in orange and glinting off of distant mountain peaks.

'I got into Hampshire College,' said Prasit suddenly.

We were leaning against the low barricade that surrounded the roof and looking up at the stars. The dark was all around us, silent and suffocating. Prasit's declaration cut through the silence like a blunt cleaver.

'I'll be leaving next August,' he said.

'Oh,' I said. 'Congratulations.'

I had applied to a few colleges in America after school, had asked for a lot of financial aid and hadn't gotten in. I had already decided on a year or two off before college. It would give me some perspective, I'd decided.

'What's happened to us, man?' I said, more to the air than to Prasit. 'You're always busy, with your girlfriend, with college applications, with work, with all kinds of things. Tara has her guys, her internship and her screwed-up family. We rarely even come here anymore.'

Prasit turned in his bed of leaves. In the complete darkness, I could barely make out his shape, his face turning towards me.

'That part is over,' he said quietly. 'We haven't listened to music together in months. We're not school kids anymore, you know? You have Rinchin, pay attention to her. I can see she really loves you.'

Prasit, my Brutus. *Et tu?* I thought the whole world was against me, against us. We were together in this. This was our ruin. This was what we were, I wanted to say. But I didn't. Instead, what I said was, 'Yeah, Rinchin does love me.'

We talked some more. But it was all unimportant. They had moved on, they weren't kids anymore. I was the only one stuck in the past, falling apart and unable to maintain myself. Maybe what growing up meant was severing old ties. Maybe that was what college would be for Prasit. A new start. He'd forget old friendships, start new ones. He'd reinvent himself, not that he needed to.

We left Boris' house at ten. The roads were relatively empty and Prasit's headlights cut through the gloom like a razor. He dropped me off outside my house and, before he sped off, turned in his seat and said, 'I'm having a small party to celebrate my admission and the scholarship. It's next Saturday. You should come.' And then he sped off, spraying dirt onto my shoes.

I had become an afterthought. Once upon a time, I would've helped plan the party. I would've organized it, invited people, and I would've been the first person Prasit would've told about his admission.

Later that night, I called Tara. She knew about Prasit's decision and his party of course. He must've just forgotten to tell you, she said glibly. We talked for an hour. Then she went to dinner. But she called back again and we talked all through the night.

'My dad's hell bent on sending me to India,' Tara said to me, almost in a whisper, as if afraid her dad might be listening at her door. 'I don't want to go. I want to stay here, go to Kathmandu University. This is where all my friends are. This is where you guys are.'

'I'm taking a year or two off,' I told her.

'I'm sorry you didn't get in anywhere,' she said instead.

'How about coming with me to Boris' tomorrow?' I asked, hoping against hope that she would come.

'Tomorrow? How about tomorrow evening? We can go to Boris' and crash at your place,' she said easily.

We were back at Boris' place the next day. Prasit came too and brought his girlfriend, a girl named Aditi who complained about everything. Prasit took her for a walk around the house and Tara and I welcomed the relief. We sat on our bed of leaves and drank our vodka.

'I don't like Aditi,' Tara said matter-of-factly.

'I don't think anyone except Prasit does,' I replied. 'Maybe she's good in bed.'

'I don't see how. She looks like she might be frigid to me,' she laughed.

'Are you a virgin?' It slipped out. It was not the way I had meant to ask. I hadn't even meant to ask.

'Why do you want to know?' she asked, smiling. 'You don't think I'd have told you?'

'I don't know,' I said. Emboldened by the alcohol, I pushed ahead, 'Would you have told me? I bet I was the last person to find out about Prasit going to Hampshire and I bet I was the last person you told about going to India. Why would that have been any different?'

Tara looked at me. Her eyes were misty but I attributed that to the alcohol. She stood and came closer, sat down next to me with my hand in hers.

It was summer, the air was cool, the wind rustling through the trees sounded like faint whispers, and there was Ruslan Vodka burning in my veins, clouding my eyes, adding what felt like an external layer to my skin, so that when Tara ran her fingers on my arm, I felt it mutedly, as if from beneath a layer of clothing. When she kissed me, she held my hands tight in hers, as if afraid they would escape.

After the kiss, she looked down her hands holding my hands. The blush never left her cheeks. I felt hollow, like her kiss had sucked out what little was left inside me. I put one arm around her shoulders and waited for her to speak.

'I'm not happy about what's happened,' she said finally.

'You don't think I've noticed? I think we all have. Prasit sees it too. He's not dumb. He probably understands it better than both of us. You know what? We're too invested in our emotions, you and me. How bad do you think things are right now? My parents are going to file for a divorce soon, I just know it. My grandfather is old and sick, I'm afraid he might die in his sleep. And I'm so afraid of leaving Nepal. I don't want to go to India. What am I going to do there? School's over now, college is starting and I don't think I can handle it. There's so much to do and so little time. Before you know it, college will be over and life will begin. It's like it's all over before it's even begun. And what do we do? We move from one thing to the other, like frogs hopping from stone to stone. We change schools, friends, jobs, partners, everything. Who's going to love me? Who's going to stay with me?'

I looked at her and she was crying, dirty rivulets staining her cheeks. I held her against me and she cried into my shirt, her tears seeping through the cotton, finding their way to my skin.

'I'll love you,' I said. 'I'll stay with you,' I whispered into her hair, muffling my words, saying them more for me than for her.

Tara looked up, wiped her cheeks with the back of her hands and smiled at me. She kissed me on the cheek and stood up to go.

I sat there for a while, not saying anything. Then I followed her down. We sat on the grass in front of the house, holding hands, tracing the lines in each other's palms. When Prasit and Aditi reappeared, I tried to let go of Tara's hand but she wouldn't. Prasit decided to drop Aditi home and head back home himself so it was only Tara who came home with me. We slept in the same bed, my arm around her, my face nestled in her hair.

The last time we visited Boris' house was almost six months later. Tara was about to leave for India, so she suggested that we go back one last time, just the three of us. After that night, the night we kissed, we hadn't gone back. Something seemed wrong, something was missing. It felt foreign.

The house was almost gone now. All the wood from the door frames and window frames had been used to build fires. The second floor was inaccessible since even the beams that we pulled ourselves up by were gone. Entire sections of the walls were missing and the forest had requisitioned the house for itself. Grass, shrubs and weeds blanketed the floor in some rooms now, growing rampant. Many of the trees that once formed the little canopy above the roof had been cut down, only their stumps left behind, like carcasses on a battlefield.

We sat outside and watched the house. It had been ours for a while. Even the junkies had recognized that. It had felt familiar, a ruin among ruins.

Tara brought out her iPod and her speakers and we listened to Bob Dylan's 'I Shall Be Released'. I sat between Tara and Prasit. Dylan's mournful voice felt naked and empty, the harmonica sounding disjointed and broken.

Tara would leave soon and so would Prasit. How long

would I stay here? I didn't know. I didn't know if I even wanted to leave. I was like Tara, afraid of the unknown, scared of what I might become if given the chance. But I had a choice, not like her, not like Prasit. Prasit was a good student, hard-working, smart and capable. It was expected of him that he go to a good school with a good scholarship in America. It didn't matter what he wanted. And I never asked him. I never asked him if he wanted to go, just assumed that he did.

When the song was over, I stood up. They looked up at me questioningly and I told them what I never had—You were my best friends.

They didn't say anything but they both stood up. We wrapped our arms around each other, our heads colliding in the middle.

'It wasn't supposed to be like this, you know?' Prasit said after a while. 'We were supposed to stick together.'

'We were,' said Tara.

I had lots to say, but it wasn't the right time. I don't know if there was or would be a right time. Either you say it or you don't. And it's the things you don't say that haunt you the most. Maybe the right time had been in that room, long ago, listening to Bob Dylan for the first time. You're all I have, I should've said. You're my friends and I love you and I'm afraid of losing you. But, of course, then it would've been too early, and now it was too late.

That was it. The last time. Tara left a few days later. Prasit a few months later. I stayed back, started work and never got around to college. I told Rinchin about that kiss with Tara and she stopped talking to me for two weeks. Eventually, after hours of apologizing and promises, we worked things out. Her condition was that I stop talking to Tara and that wasn't too difficult, seeing as how Tara was in India, in college and with new friends. Rinchin and I were happy together, at least for a while. Then things changed once again and she left me. It was really all my fault.

I saw Tara and Prasit on their holidays from college. They'd bring back stories about their escapades and I'd listen to them all, sharing little in return. Nothing much happens in Kathmandu.

Two

'It is so wearisome. First you put on your shirt, then your trousers; you drag yourself into bed at night and in the morning, drag yourself out again; and always you put one foot in front of the other. There is little hope that it will ever change. Millions have always done it like that and millions more will do so after us. Moreover, since we're made up of two halves which both do the same thing, everything's done twice. It's all very boring and very, very sad.'

—Georg Büchner, *Danton's Death*

All Anam saw that night was the sky, spread out like an inky canvas strewn with points of fire-like paint. He did recall stepping off the pavement but did not smell the pungent acridity of burning rubber, did not feel the asphalt hard and unyielding on his back, nor did he hear the slow whine of the car engine as it ground to a stop, the pattering of many feet or the hushed din of whispering voices. He did not recognize the man who stepped into his field of vision, obscuring the stars, the likes of which he had never seen before. He did not feel the man's pasty white hand as it slid under his shirt collar, feeling around for his pulse, and he did not feel the blood, warm and

thick, flow from his left ear, pooling behind his head like a
halo. He did not taste the sharp metal of iron as more blood
leaked from the corners of his paralyzed mouth. He did not
register the stabbing hurt of his broken nose, the lung
punctured by a jagged rib, and even his sputtering heart,
beating and beating against his chest like a war drum. He did
not hear the woman next to him keep repeating, 'Hare Ram,
Hare Ram.' All Anam saw was the sky—clear, boundless
night.

Earlier that day Anam had woken from uneasy dreams to the
sharp ringing of his Chinese alarm clock. He brushed leisurely
and shaved with a Gillette double-bladed razor. He put on a
brown suit, a red tie, and polished his shoes, just like he did
every day. He left his rented room in Baneshwor and walked
down the street to the local eatery where he ate a bowl of
thukpa with a fried egg on top. There was a man sitting at the
table next to him, reading *Kantipur*. Anam glanced over at the
paper and, although he couldn't see it, the headline said—Bus
bombed in Badarmude, at least thirty dead. Anam ate quickly,
paid his bill and left, stopping for a cigarette at a paan-pasal,
chatting briefly with the storekeeper. The man was chewing
betel while talking to Anam, occasionally turning his head
ninety degrees to spit out a stream of red, viscous liquid.
Anam flinched unconsciously, worried the spit might splatter
onto him, but kept up the conversation, remarking on the
load-shedding hours and the queues for petrol.

Anam smoked half his cigarette, then carefully ground the lit end against the brick pavement and slipped it into his breast pocket, saving it for later. The storekeeper, watching, called Anam over. Slipping two loose Suryas into Anam's shirt pocket, the man smiled widely, exposing teeth reddish-brown from tobacco and paan. Anam thanked him profusely and walked away. A few hours later, realizing that he'd given Anam the last two cigarettes from his pack, the storekeeper would tear open a new pack, only to have them burst out into the street as if alive. He would spend the next ten minutes hunting here and there for the twenty cigarettes and bitterly regret giving Anam his last two from the previous pack.

Near the alleyway by the Birendra International Convention Centre, Anam waved to Akriti from across the street. She was wearing a sleeveless white kurta and a matching churidar. Akriti lifted herself on tiptoes as she waved back, but there was no smile on her face and her eyes were dark. Anam didn't know there was something wrong with Akriti until the moment she shied from his embrace. He reached for her hand and she let him hold it but did not reciprocate his insistent grip. They walked awkwardly, she leading him through a crowd and he trying not to let go. She stopped at a park bench not too far from the street and they sat down side by side. Akriti did not look at him, only down at her hands, folded together in her lap. Anam had been forced to let go as they sat. He asked her what was wrong but she only sighed.

Behind them was the park and there came sounds of a shuttlecock being tossed around. Two middle-aged women in saris were daintily lobbing the badminton shuttlecock back and forth, barely exerting themselves. Beyond them a young teenager, his hair long and unkempt, wearing a Nirvana T-shirt, played with a gigantic Tibetan mastiff, holding a stick out to it as it jumped around. Anam did not listen to much music and so ignored tinny Aruna Lama playing out of a scratchy radio three stories up.

Anam looked at Akriti. 'What happened to us?' she asked quietly. Anam did not reply. He did not think there was anything wrong. He searched her face for a clue but she remained impassive, betraying no emotion. There were dark circles under her eyes, as if she hadn't slept, and her fingers were knotted and tangled in her lap.

'I can't do this anymore,' she said, more to herself than to him. '*Ma sakdina…*'

The slump of her shoulders told Anam all he needed to know. He saw determination but not the little sadness. She had made up her mind long before coming to see him. She had made up her mind last night as they had argued on the phone over whether or not she was spending too much time with her friend Sarthak. Three hours before her conversation with Anam, while on the phone with Sarthak, Akriti had decided to break up with Anam. But last night, during their conversation, Anam had been distracted, seemingly not interested in what she had to say. She had felt a little bad for him and so had set up a meeting the next day. After hanging up, Akriti had called Sarthak back and reported what had happened. Sarthak was angry at first, blaming her for wanting to stay with Anam and not be with him, but she managed to calm him down and they spent the next two hours talking dirty on the phone. Sarthak touched himself while Akriti acted coy. She slept little that night.

Anam watched as the teenager with the dog threw a stick into the air, but the mastiff stared back dumbly, its tongue lolling and tail thumping happily. Anam turned back to Akriti as she looked down at her hands again. He sighed slowly, letting out the air and deflating his lungs. Akriti reached over and clutched his right hand.

'*Ma janchu hai?*' Akriti said slowly, more a statement than a request. 'I have to go.'

Anam nodded and extracted his hand from hers. He stood just as she did.

'I'll call you,' Akriti said, already walking away. A candy wrapper crunched under her sandals, the teenager with the dog was trying to make the mastiff follow him, a couple walked arm-in-arm towards Akriti but separated to let her pass between them. Anam's palms were sweaty and he wiped them on his thighs, a hollowness in the pit of his stomach. He wondered if it was sadness or just hunger.

The couple who'd parted for Akriti passed by Anam as he stood contemplating where to go for lunch. They walked down the street, hand-in-hand, her body lodged comfortably against his. Unlike Anam's recently deceased relationship, theirs was like laligurans in full bloom. They had met in high school, dated for a year, then broken up and dated other people. But once locking lips with another, they realized how much they missed each other, and promptly got back together. It had been ten years now, and her palm had lines on it from washing dishes and his back constantly made cracking noises from the construction job. Their Dhapasi flat was small, cramped and dark but the walls were painted a bright summery yellow. Her choice. Together with Anam, they boarded a microbus to New Road. Anam sat in the back while the two sat in the front seat, their four legs tangled.

Anam got off the microbus at Thamel where his office was. At his desk he found a stack of folders, each consisting of a couple hundred bills and receipts. The invoices and bills needed to go into one pile, the receipts into another. They needed to be checked, one by one, the item and amount noted down in a ledger and organized by date. Repeat for each pile, then repeat for each folder. While the office around him bustled with activity, Anam did not talk to anyone for the first two hours of his shift.

At 11.30 a.m., he took a break. He walked to the bathroom, carefully avoiding people he might have to speak to. Manish waved at him from across the office and, for a second, Anam was afraid he would walk over and make small talk. Fortunately, Manish bent back down to his computer and Anam slipped into the bathroom. He stood at the urinal for about thirty seconds and then washed his hands at the sink. The hand towel hanging next to the sink was black with dirt, so Anam chose to wipe his hands on his pants and exit the bathroom.

Halfway to his cubicle, Esha reached out from hers and grabbed his hand. Anam jumped and made a little sound but it was only Esha, so he smiled nervously. Esha returned his smile and asked him how he was. Anam made sounds, more or less words, and mumbled a lot. Esha played with a stray strand of her matted black hair, not quite dreadlocks yet, as she listened to Anam. She was head designer for the company and was working on a new logo. She showed Anam her early models and Anam smiled and nodded at the right moments. Anam noted the slight tan of her neck compared to the skin of her chest. He noted that the green logo she was now showing him looked vaguely familiar. Although Anam himself could not recall where he had seen the symbol before, it was identical to that of Peugeot, the French car manufacturer.

Esha had worked on the green logo for close to two days now, it was the one she liked best. She had missed her best friend's birthday celebration because of that damn logo. She had called exactly at midnight but her best friend was already drunk, yelling and laughing maniacally. Although Esha wanted desperately to tell her about the crush that she had had on her since late middle school, she swallowed the lump in her throat and yelled a happy birthday before hanging up.

Anam managed to extract himself from Esha's attentions and walked back to his cubicle. He worked for another two hours on a folder and, like every other day, left exactly at 1 p.m. for his lunch break. Anam deliberated on where to eat for quite some time, since he was down to his last five hundred rupees. He debated blowing the majority of his money on a good hot meal, maybe a thali at that fancy place in Lainchaur. He would have lots of white rice, thick daal, local chicken gravy, fried cauliflower and potato, saag and mula ko achar. Instead he decided to lunch at the local family-run eatery like he did every day. He did not order, for there was no need. The proprietor's eldest daughter, who Anam thought was fifteen when in reality she was eighteen, brought him his usual order—

a plate of white rice, a small container of lean, watery chicken curry and a plate of very spicy chilli potatoes. He ate without relish, so completely used to the taste that he did not savour it anymore, simply chewing like a machine, so-so number of times, and swallowing.

He smoked the remaining half of the cigarette that he had saved and watched out of the corner of his eye as one of the young interns from the creative department devoured a stack of rotis and container after container of the bean and potato curry. Opposite the boy sat two women from the creative department, both of whom he worked with regularly, and they, like him, watched the young intern eat the rotis. After twelve rotis the intern stopped, leaned back in his chair and took a long, deep swallow from his Coke bottle. He slammed the bottle down on the table and belched loudly. The two women looking on laughed heartily. One of them glanced over in Anam's direction, caught his eye, but quickly looked away before Anam could initiate a smile.

Anam waited at the table until it was five minutes to two, then stood up and walked over to pay the bill. Smiling, he slid a fifty rupee note to the proprietor's daughter. She picked up the note with her right hand and rubbed her neck unconsciously with the left, the same spot where her boyfriend had hit her two days ago while they were having furtive sex behind the garage where he worked as a mechanic. Her boyfriend was ten years older and had a bad temper. He viewed an occasional slap or two as part of the privilege afforded to him as the boyfriend. Three days from now the proprietor would find out about his daughter's lover and forbid her from ever seeing him again. She would leave that very night, taking with her what little possessions she had and thirteen thousand rupees from her father's strongbox. Her boyfriend would hide her in his rented room down by the bus-park at Kalanki and forbid her from leaving the room without him. For three days she would wait for him until he got home after dark, drunk and abusive. He would have rough sex with her, often slapping her around, and then go to sleep. After the third day, she would go back to her father, taking what little remained of the thirteen thousand rupees from her boyfriend's pants pocket.

Anam took his hands out of his pockets as he sat back down at his cubicle. He played Solitaire for a while, starting a new game each time he felt he was about to fail. He thought of calling his mother in Biratnagar, as he hadn't talked to her in maybe eight months, but decided against it. He played with his tie, the laces of his shoes and the lobe of his ears. He checked his email periodically, refreshing the page again and again every few seconds, hoping something interesting would come through. He leafed through a women's magazine that only featured socialites and thought about calling Akriti, but then remembered she had just broken up with him. He thought about calling Sushant but then remembered Sushant had left to work at an IT firm in Dubai (it had been a year). He thought about calling Ramesh but then remembered Ramesh had left to do his MBA in China (it had been eight months). Anam looked through the address book of his non-functional mobile phone, disconnected for non-payment. There was no one he could call and make small talk with. There was no one he could even make plans to have some tea with. He thought about calling Akriti.

By the time it was five, Anam had finished organizing three of the seven folders. He neatly folded up the remaining folders and placed them inside a binder, inside the top left drawer of his desk. He adjusted the position of the phone, which must've moved when he'd made and received a call or two. He wiped the computer screen and replaced the protective cover on the keyboard. He made sure everything was turned off, except for his answering machine and fax, stood up, straightened his tie, made sure his room keys were in his pocket, and left the building.

Outside, he felt an insane craving for some samosas. Although he knew he shouldn't spend any more money frivolously, Anam decided that the samosas would be his dinner.

Dodging people along the narrow alleyway to Tip-Top Tailors and, furtively hidden behind it, Tip-Top Samosas, Anam felt his mouth water as the smell of fried dough and potatoes wafted through the air. He thought of the sweet red achar, the hot, scalding samosas and a cool dudh-malai to wash it all down. The first bite of his samosa burnt the roof of his mouth and Anam opened his mouth and breathed out furiously, switching the mouthful from side to side.

A woman with hair down to her waist watched Anam from the opposite corner as he struggled to eat. She sat at a table, smiling to herself, revelling in his discomfort. Anam saw her smile but looked away before she could meet his eyes. The woman with the long hair shifted her weight from her left foot to her right, ruffling her sari in the process. She reached down and adjusted the numerous folds, her glass bangles clinking a haphazard melody. There were shopping bags around her feet, five in total, crammed with clothes and boxes. She had been shopping for the family. It was early shopping for Dashain and Dashain meant new clothes for everyone. While looking for new shoes for herself, she'd tried on a pair of three-inch-high black pumps. The salesman had put them on her feet himself, slowly lifting the hem of her sari to expose her ankles. He had then leaned back, crouched on his haunches, a smile playing on his lips and his head nodding as he surveyed her feet. She had stood, holding her sari up as she too surveyed her ankles, noticing for the first time the shape of her calves. When the salesman had taken the pumps off, he had run his fingers down the length of her feet, almost caressing them. The woman with the long hair had felt an involuntary shiver and almost held out a hand to stop him but it was over before it even began and she wondered if it had happened at all.

Anam watched as the woman with the long hair finished her lassi, carefully picked up her five bags and walked out smartly on three-inch-high black pumps. He finished the rest of his meal in silence and in his own company.

Anam usually went home straight after work, but the samosas rested comfortably in his stomach and he felt content. He wondered what had caused the samosa craving this particular day and felt a little uneasy; his daily routine disturbed, he felt as if the world was shifting. He wondered if it was just the sweet sauce he'd ingested or something else entirely that was making him sweat, despite his apparent contentment. He made his way to Tundikhel and chose a clean spot to lie on the grass. He removed his coat and folded it carefully before placing it under his head as a pillow. It was getting darker and Anam could see a faint crescent moon in the sky. There were wispy clouds conglomerating and a chill in the air despite the summer. Anam recalled waking up uneasy that day, feeling utterly and completely desolate. He closed his eyes and thought about the dream he had had last night.

Anam had been sitting on the ground cross-legged with a banana-leaf plate before him. A woman entered the room with a big pot of rice. She scooped out a huge ladleful onto his banana leaf. There was another woman behind her and another and another, each with a pot full of either daal, tarkari or achar. Each ladled generous portions onto his plate. Anam ate ravenously, relishing the food. When he finished one plateful, the women brought more. Anam kept eating, never sated, but growing increasingly sick of the food. It reminded him strongly of all that his mother used to make when he was a child, each and every day for lunch and dinner. Anam tried to call out to the women, to tell them to bring him some mutton maybe, or some fish, or even rotis would do. Just something other than this bhaat, daal, kukhura, tarkari and achar. But he couldn't say a word. Each time he tried to speak, a piece of food fell from his mouth. First it was a piece of chicken, whole, cooked and edible. He tried again to speak and warm white rice fell out this time. He tried again and choked on the liquid daal that leaked from his mouth and nose. And, all the while, the women kept piling his banana leaf with food and his right hand kept moving, as if on its own, shovelling mouthful after mouthful into his mouth. He couldn't talk. All he could do

was eat. He chewed and swallowed, yearning with each bite
for something different, anything to break the monotony,
maybe a burger, momos, some chowmein. The scene repeated
itself. Anam retched inwardly, the food now tasting
horrendous, like rotten eggs and meat; it smelled like vomit
each time he brought a mouthful to his face. And yet he
couldn't stop eating. After endless repetition Anam mercifully
woke, the alarm his saviour.

Disturbed by the memory, Anam opened his eyes and
looked off to the side, beyond the grass and the metal fence
surrounding Tundikhel and there, by the road, underneath
the pedestrian overhead bridge, an old man sat on a bench,
tending two portable stoves. On one stove was a pot of tea
that he stirred continuously with a steel ladle and on the
other, a pan that he was frying an egg on. The old man had
been tending the same roadside stall for thirteen years now. It
provided him with a sense of purpose. He loved the cooking,
the spare simple ingredients of his food and the regulars who
frequented his stall. And though he always got to the same
spot at 7 a.m. every morning, unzipped the bags strapped to
his creaky old bicycle and set up the portable stoves on the
sidewalk in exactly the same way, he did it with pleasure every
day. For, despite the regular repetition, each day was different,
each day was something new simply because of the day that
had preceded it. Every morning he made his signature noodle
spice—a blend of red and green chilli, garlic, ginger, lemon
and finely chopped red onions, and each time he tasted it, it
tasted slightly different, depending on what he had eaten the
night before, how much sleep he had had, the weather, the

position of the sun in the sky, the phase of the moon or the state of his own creaky back.

Anam got onto a microbus parked underneath the pedestrian overhead bridge, near the old man with his stoves. He sat in the first row at the window and looked out. There was a man on a motorcycle with a woman sitting sideways behind him. There was a small child, maybe five or six years of age, her hair in pigtails, sitting in between them, her tiny arms around her father's waist. Her mother's braided hair flew like a kite tail behind her as the motorcycle zoomed in and out of Kathmandu traffic. The family was headed to a birthday party for the man's boss' son. The man on the motorcycle had picked out a G.I. Joe toy for the seven-year-old's birthday. It had cost him four hundred rupees at the supermarket. While there, he had also bought a Snickers bar, a bottle of Coke which he had proceeded to drink then and there, and a Gillette Mach 3 razor he would later use to shave the hair off his chest, which his wife had wryly commented on last night. Anam watched as the man's red helmet disappeared from view as his microbus took a right at Jamal.

At Kala's house, Anam pressed the doorbell and it was Kala's mother who opened the door. Kala's mother brought a cup of tea for Anam and he waited at the table while Kala turned off the television and collected her books. Over the next hour, Anam taught Kala trigonometry, although he had never really been very good at mathematics while in school. People didn't care that he hadn't exactly studied mathematics in college; they assumed that any young man who had gone to college in America was qualified to teach mathematics to a

Class 9 student. Anam sipped his tea and talked to Kala in sin, cos and tan.

Towards the end of their session, Kala asked Anam about college and Anam told her the same thing that he'd been telling everyone else since he'd returned seven years ago—he wasn't the right person to ask. Look at me, he would say, I went to America on a full scholarship, out in Kansas in the middle of nowhere. I've been out of college for years now and I don't have a decent job, a decent place to live, no money saved up, no car, no motorcycle, not even a bicycle, no girlfriend and no interests. Sure, he'd read J Krishnamurti in college, but that didn't necessarily translate into a job in Nepal. (People in Kathmandu were more into Osho than Krishnamurti anyway.) He'd taken a few economics classes and those had helped land him a menial job in the finance department of a failing ad company and somehow he'd managed to con Kala's family into letting him take her mathematics tuition. 'Don't ask me,' Anam really wanted to say to young Kala. 'I'm the one who failed without even trying.'

Anam said goodbye to Kala at the door. She watched Anam walk down the driveway and only after he had disappeared from view did she step back into the house and shut the door. The phone rang and Kala ran for it, elbowing her father out of the way. It was her Uncle Dinesh, asking for her father. Kala handed the phone over, disappointed. Kala had kissed a boy for the first time three days back. He had called her each night since then and today was the first time that he had been late. Kala had been afraid the phone would ring during her tuition with Anam and her father would answer it and she would have to explain to him who the boy calling for her was. She wouldn't have known what to say, except that the boy looked a little like Anam.

Outside, Anam turned the corner and stopped for a cigarette. He took a drag, flicked the cigarette and blew out the smoke. He felt a little sick. It wasn't a physical pain, just a nausea that seemed to start not in his stomach but his diaphragm. He finished the cigarette and crushed the butt beneath his heel. He spat to the side of the street and walked about a hundred feet to an intersection. Night had fallen suddenly while Anam had been teaching Kala trigonometric conversion. There was a faint, almost artificial smell of lilac in the air. It was summer but strangely chilly, the wind rising and falling in waves, like in the autumn. We call it 'autumn', thought Anam, but they call it 'fall'. He waited at the intersection to cross the street. He looked left and right and was about to step onto the street when he saw headlights approaching in the distance. Anam noticed the car was moving fast. With his foot almost off the edge, the moment seemed to lengthen into an eternity and there, hovering between blacktop and pavement, Anam made a decision.

As the car driven by the man with the pasty skin rushed towards him, Anam stepped back from the street, back onto the pavement. He looked up at the sky, spread out like a canvas strewn with points of fire-like paint. Tendrils of smoke floated into the night, an errant column from someone's nearby cigarette. Headlights washed over him as Anam stood frozen, gazing up at the night sky. He didn't notice the car swerve erratically. The car careened wildly to the side, its tires howling on the blacktop. It climbed onto the pavement and crashed into a wall, bending its hood in half and leaking black smoke from its engine.

Seconds later, Anam was kneeling next to the man with the pasty skin, having just dragged him from the wreckage of the car. His eyes were open and staring but his mouth made gasping, drowning noises. Anam felt for the man's pulse but even as Anam counted the beats, twenty-one, twenty-two, twenty-three, twenty-four, they spluttered, foundered and eventually stopped. With his hand on the dead man's wrist, Anam thought of what might have been instead, a punctured lung and a halo of blood. Anam felt a tug, as if he were on the back of a motorcycle making a sharp turn. His body wanted to keep going in one direction but the world had irrevocably taken a turn. A crowd of people had gathered, someone was taking pictures with a mobile phone and a woman next to him repeated 'Hare Ram, Hare Ram' over and over again.

Maya

Maya watched the box with interest, a steady ticking emanating from the recesses of the brown container. There were no labels, no marks, just an innocuous cardboard box wrapped clumsily in coarse brown paper. The folds were messy, the creases everywhere. Maya picked it up and shook it gently. A slight clattering. So something small, maybe mechanical, she thought. A clock? A bomb?

The man who had left the box at her counter hadn't looked like a Maoist, but nowadays Maoists came in all colours. (Why, only yesterday she'd heard those glue-sniffing street kids from around the corner threaten some fancy teenagers saying they were members of the Maoist party. The teenagers, dressed in jeans too loose for their hips, T-shirts two sizes too big, and caps with flat, wide brims, pushed the street kids aside casually, barely even acknowledging them.)

The man, anyway, the man. He was tall, a fair man, with wide cheeks and prominent bones. He had a craggy complexion, like the side of a rock exposed to swift winds. And he had smiled; smiled while he took the box out of his bag—a ratty-looking thing with frayed straps and a zipper that looked like a mouth with bad teeth. Maya remembered his hands, how smooth they'd been, even the palms, like a virgin piece of slate, so unlike his face. There was no hair on his knuckles, not even his forearms. He cradled the box in his hands for a second before he put it on the counter and slid it over. Maya tried to remember, had it been ticking then?

'For Ramesh,' he'd said in the deepest voice she'd ever heard. For a moment she imagined what it would be like to have that voice whisper in her ear, dark things, things she would gladly do if that voice just asked her.

Maya shook the box again, slower this time, hoping not to set off a bomb (if one was inside). Now this Ramesh, he wasn't a very straight fellow, but surely not the terrorist type. He came here often and usually left things for others to pick up, always with a generous tip for Maya. But she wondered often about Ramesh. He had once taken her to a bhatti for beer and then, in the darkness and in his drunkenness, tried to grope her. The first few times, she'd let him.

Ramesh reminded Maya of a mongoose, or some kind of rodent at least. He spoke too fast, often too fast for Maya to clearly understand what he was saying. He wore coats two sizes too big and Maya was almost certain they were stolen. Or maybe they were just his brother's hand-me-downs.

Maya was still trying to conjure up Ramesh in her mind when he appeared before her like a pichaas. 'Maya baini, *kasto cha timlai?*' he asked, too fast.

'I'm okay, Ramesh dai, just a little tired from yesterday,' she replied.

'Yesterday? What happened yesterday?' Ramesh was immediately curious, as Maya was certain he would be.

'Oh, nothing really. Just a few of the girls got together for a little party at that bhatti. It was Ramila's birthday and we all got a little drunk.'

'Ramila? My Ramila? Our Ramila? Why wasn't I invited?' Little things excited Ramesh so.

'It was for girls only, kya,' Maya said sweetly, flirting openly.

'I need to get a gift for Ramila then,' Ramesh said. 'Our Ramila. How old is she now?'

'She's eighteen. But you don't need to buy her a gift. Everyone already gave their gifts. If you buy her something now, she'll know that you forgot her birthday.'

'Forgot! I didn't even know!' said Ramesh, flustered.

He turned away, towards the street, and appeared lost in thought, head bowed and hands fidgeting. He looked so much like an anthropomorphic mongoose, even from the back. Maya knew exactly what he was doing. 'Here!' He swiveled suddenly and slapped a few notes on the counter. Three hundred rupees. 'One for you and two for Ramila. Tell her that it's from me.'

Maya smiled. She fingered the box, her fingers flitting over the brown wrapping and lingering on the inexpert folds and creases. She thought she could still feel a ticking. She wanted to ask but refrained. The reason Ramesh always came back to her was because she never asked.

'I'm off,' said Ramesh, before Maya could even bring up the box. He reached over and squeezed Maya's hand before scampering away. Maya let him go, holding on to the box for now.

Maya folded the three notes and slid them into her bra. Poor Ramesh. There was no Ramila. There never had been any Ramila. Once, one of the girls, maybe it was Radha, had had a visitor. A tall, fair girl, dressed in a salwar-kurta. This was a long, white kurta, patterned and expensive, the kind that Maya could never afford. Her hair had been long, but done up in a confining bun and laced with streaks of red. She'd smelled of fresh flowers, as if she'd just taken a bath. Maya had almost melted with jealousy.

Ramesh had appeared at that exact moment to collect an envelope. Maya didn't like envelopes. She couldn't read and the most she could do with an envelope was smell it. Ramesh's letters never smelled like anything, except for a faint odour of sweat. Ramesh had seen the new girl, that beautiful girl. That girl, whoever she was, became Ramila.

The other girls kept up the charade once they were let in on the secret. Each time Ramesh asked after Ramila, they came up with some elaborate tale. So Ramila fell sick with alarming regularity. Her family members passed away, one after another, in the course of the past three months, and even all her clothes had been stolen by the washerman. Ramila never had enough money for medicine. She didn't have money to go back home to see her dead family. She didn't have money to buy new clothes. Ramesh thought he loved Ramila, even though he'd just seen her once, and Ramesh always had money.

Maya luxuriated behind the counter, happy with the three hundred she had made just by standing around. It was a slow afternoon, not much happening on the streets outside. Sometimes there would be an incident. The massage parlour opposite got busted with alarming frequency. The woman who ran it thought she was above the law because she had once slept with Deepak Manange, so she didn't pay off the cops. The cops conducted periodic raids and the parlour's girls always seemed to get taken in. And everyone knows what those thieving police do once they have you in that van. Pretty girls come back looking like ghosts, many can't walk straight for days.

Maya thought a lot about the Rato Bhaley getting busted too. She imagined a police officer breaking down the door while she was in there with a customer. What would happen to her? Would the police do with her what they did with all the other girls? And how would she feel? Would she feel anything even? After all, how different would it be from what she did every day?

If ever arrested, things would be worse for her, Maya knew. She knew she was a pretty girl. Her hair was thick, although frayed at the ends; her cheekbones were high and her eyes small. She had a naturally petite body, never seeming to gain weight, the envy of all the other girls. It infuriated them that customers almost always asked for Maya. She was fair, not white like the kuirey tourists that frequented Thamel, but like dirty porcelain. Maya, however, had a lot of scars and customers didn't like scars. Scars meant accidents, scars meant disease.

One particular scar bothered her more than the others. A deep, long mass of scar tissue ran all the way from the inside of her right thigh to her belly button, like a deep, winding river. Maya didn't like to think about it but that was the one most customers always asked about. She'd tell them that she'd fallen down a cliff when she was a child. A stray branch had torn her thigh wide open as she'd careened down the slope. Most believed her.

Maya adjusted herself in her chair, running her hands through her long hair. As she watched the street, a little girl walked past, in a blue school uniform with red ribbons tied to her pigtails. She carried a backpack, sagging and frayed towards the bottom. Maya spied a brown book edge poking out. The girl looked exceedingly like Manju. Maybe it was the pigtails or the red ribbons but Maya was reminded of Manju with a suddenness that was frightening.

Manju, little sister Manju, oh how Maya missed her! As fair as Maya, only prettier. Manju was six when Maya left, a sweet little girl in pigtails that bounced every time she ran. Whenever Maya looked at her, she felt love so simple and so strong, it left her helpless. Maya wanted a good life for Manju. She wanted Manju to go to school and get married to a nice man. That was one of the reasons Maya had left. She wanted to make enough money to send Manju to school, to Plus Two, maybe even for her BA. Leaving her behind was the hardest thing Maya had ever done. Cold, heartless Kathmandu was no place for a girl like Manju. But it was in cold heartless Kathmandu that Maya missed Manju most.

Maya often thought of writing to her family, and maybe she would've if she'd just known to read and write. But she couldn't trust any of the other girls with her thoughts. She already felt naked around them and didn't want to bare even her mind to them. She missed her old father, whose bones ached like wildfire every winter, and her mother with her prolapsed uterus. Maya had never witnessed anything as horrible as her mother's affliction. Just two days before she left home, she'd taken her ailing mother to the travelling health camp. There she'd watched as the doctors, in green foreign caps, inspected her mother's uterus, protruding sickly out of her vagina. The doctors were afraid to operate as Maya's mother had blood conditions, so all they did was push the uterus back in and plug it up. Maya's mother didn't mind much. After all, she'd been living with the condition for six years, ever since Manju had been born. And she'd walked for two days to reach the health camp.

It was three in the afternoon when a commotion outside jolted Maya out of her reverie. A glue-sniffing khate had been begging money from a pretty female tourist. She had been eating a sandwich, which she had tried to give to the boy. The boy grabbed the sandwich and the camera she'd been holding. He tried to run but realized too late that the lady had the camera strap around her hand. In a few seconds, shopkeepers had gathered around to protect this lovely lady. Gawkers added to the mix, and pretty soon this little khate was being slapped around. He started to cry, snot leaking from his nose in long tendrils, his left hand still holding the half-eaten sandwich. The woman tried to look stern but Maya could see that she was getting uncomfortable with the beatings. The police showed up a few minutes later. Batons out, they cleared the rabble, got hold of the boy, apologized profusely to the foreign lady and then eyed her ass as she walked away hurriedly.

This kuirey lady had long blonde hair in a ponytail, a massive backpack and dark sunglasses that hid her eyes and covered most of her face. The camera still dangled from her right hand. Maya wondered if the lady's eyes were as blue as deep, clean water, like some of the other white people's. She kept a running count of all her white customers. She'd had four, and only one of them had blue eyes. If she ever had a child, she wanted him to have blue eyes.

By four in the afternoon, Maya had taken in four other packages and three envelopes, and given away all of them except for a letter. Usually letters went fast, faster than most packages. They were often delivered by doe-eyed boys and picked up by dew-eyed girls. Maya enjoyed romances, and knew that these little pieces of paper spoke of unyielding love and unfaltering devotion. Maya couldn't read, so she didn't know for sure, but the other girls often tore open the envelopes. Maybe another reason why most trusted Maya with their deliveries.

The packages, though, were always mysteries. Each time someone new delivered a package, Maya would create elaborate backstories. Some were jealous lovers and the boxes contained parts of their rivals, killed and wrapped to be delivered. Others were drug dealers and the packages contained vast amounts of cocaine, the only drug Maya had ever tried. A customer, a white man, had once brought some over. He wanted her to try it but Maya had protested. She didn't know what it was, and she sure wasn't putting anything that looked like salt up her nose. The foreigner had been convincing, and eventually cajoled Maya into agreeing. Maya had sneezed but the cocaine had been delightful. A throb of pleasure had coursed through her body, leaving her wanting more and more out of the customer. He had laughed.

Maya knew her place and she knew her job. Twenty days of the month she was at work and the rest of the ten days she sat at the counter, playing the postwoman. People shuffled in and out frequently. Those who left packages were transients, except for people like Ramesh, who were regulars. Letters were usually always from local boys and girls, those who couldn't meet openly, for fear of fathers with guns and mothers with prejudices.

When Maya first arrived at the Rato Bhaley Dance Bar and Massage Parlor, Sarita had been at the counter, sitting on an old bamboo chair, one hand inside her kurta, scratching her thigh. Maya had asked if they were looking for waitresses. Maya knew they weren't looking for waitresses. Sarita had looked at her long and hard, one of those stares that Maya had come to detest so much. It was the look people gave you when they were visualizing you naked.

Two hours and one conversation later Maya had the job. Basanta dai had been kind, as kind as could be expected. He wanted a 50 per cent cut on whatever they earned, that was it. They could keep all tips. Just one condition though. Maya would have to spend ten days at the counter, just like all the other girls. Sarita would explain everything to her. And Sarita did explain everything, just not enough. Maya didn't know why they operated the counter, as she never handed in any money from the counter to Basanta dai. But Maya knew when to stop asking.

The girls alternated. First was Radha, then Rama, Sarita and finally Maya. All of them sat at the counter when they had their periods, and a few days after too. All of them knew their place, but Maya knew best of all. For Maya life wasn't a game, but the packages were. She knew her job, hated what she did, but did it because she had little choice. What other job could a poor uneducated girl from the villages ever get in a city like Kathmandu? Besides waiting tables, washing dishes and this, what else was there? At least this paid the most. The packages were a diversion and maybe that was why she so enjoyed her time behind the counter. For ten days she could pretend to be someone else.

It had been almost a year now. She missed her family with an ache that was pervasive and terminal. She cried alone at night, stifling sobs into her dirty pillow. At first she kept telling herself that the Rato Bhaley was temporary, until she raised enough money to go back home, to send Manju to school, to take care of her parents. Now, almost a year later, Maya had little money saved up. She made a modest amount, even after Basanta dai's cut, but most of it went towards food and rent. She lived in a cramped apartment in Chettrapati, just a fifteen-minute walk from Thamel. Chettrapati was seedy, especially the area she lived in. Junkies, thieves and murderers waited at every corner. She'd already been robbed twice. Her apartment had a single bedroom where three other girls slept. Maya slept in the living room, on a simple cot with a bone-thin mattress. They shared a single toilet, which was almost always flooded. The other girls often shared Maya's clothes. Maya made more money than them, so she would end up buying more clothes.

She didn't mind sharing as long as they gave it back. Some did, most didn't.

It wasn't just her clothes, her money often went missing as well. She tried her hardest not to lend money and hid whatever she had in a sock and under her mattress. Thrice, a few hundred rupees had disappeared from the sock. As much as she hated to leave her money there, she was loath to carry it with her, always afraid of having it stolen.

Seven o'clock and the one letter still remained. Maya didn't know what to do with it. Usually the people who delivered the letters said who they were for, but this one man, he'd just handed it over and slunk away, like a rat into the darkness. The letter was an old-fashioned white envelope with red borders, two faded stamps peeling in one corner.

'Oi Maya! We're going home. *Aira ho?*' shouted Radha, busy changing clothes.

'There's still one left.' Maya turned the letter over in her hands, feeling the coarse paper with her fingertips, imagining what secrets lay in its lettered depths.

'Let me see,' said Sarita, whom Maya secretly hated, and snatched the letter from her hands. Sarita was short, a plump woman with breasts like sacks of rice and a girth wider than a peepal tree. Plus Sarita could read.

'Oho!' Sarita exclaimed in surprise. 'This letter is for you!'

'What?' Maya didn't believe her for a second. In another second, all of the girls had gathered around the letter. Maya believed her then.

'It says so right here. Written in such nice handwriting.'

'What does it say? Read it quick!' said Rama, more excited than Maya was.

As Sarita tore the letter open, Maya flinched. Inside was a single sheet of paper, lined notebook paper torn from a school copybook. 'Mero pyari Maya...' Sarita began. And suddenly Maya didn't want to hear anymore. She knew what the letter contained. Only her mother, who thought she was a waitress, knew where she worked in Kathmandu. She'd only sent one letter home. A single sheet of paper with one solitary paragraph, dictated by her and written down by Sarita, which said she worked at the Rato Bhaley in Thamel.

'Stop...' Maya mumbled.

Sarita paused. Her face went slack, the corners of her too-wide mouth began to droop. Radha, who had passed Class 6, read over her shoulder. Maya knew. Maya didn't want to know.

'Maya...' began Radha.

'Don't tell me!' Maya screamed. She knew it. The letter would be the end of everything. Something dark lived in those words that Maya couldn't read. She wanted to be somewhere else, someone else.

'But...' the others protested.

'Chup! All of you! I don't want to know!'

Her father had died, her sister had died, her entire family had perished in a landslide, in a flood, in the war, murdered by the Maoists, slaughtered by the army, her mother had a fatal sickness, her father was dying, Manju was sick, Manju had been raped and killed by the army, Manju had been raped by four men, three army men and one other man from her village, raped and slit with a hunting knife all the way from thigh to belly button, Manju had bled and bled and bled but her father had taken her to the health post in time, Manju now had a scar running from her thigh to her belly button like a deep winding river, Manju had run away to Kathmandu unable to bear the shame, Manju had contemplated killing herself, Manju now sold herself at the Rato Bhaley.

Maya clamped her hands on her ears, trying to blot out the world. She shut her eyes, squeezed them until tears as hot as blood leaked from their sides. Radha put her arm around Maya and Maya fell to the ground. 'The bomb, the bomb,' Maya mumbled.

'What bomb?' Radha asked, concern lining her seventeen-year-old face. 'It'll be alright. We're here for you.'

'The bomb,' said Maya again.

'What bomb…' began Sarita before Rama hushed her.

'The package,' Maya said more to herself than anyone else. 'That bomb, it should have just exploded.'

Knife in the Water

She watched him. He was sitting rigid, his body angled awkwardly and his legs askew. He was sitting closer to the television, in that gaudy green armchair that She hated. When She brought the whisky in, He seized the glass reflexively, an action He had repeated countless times before. She moved to get back to the kitchen but He reached out towards her. She flinched and He motioned for her to sit on the couch opposite him. She complied, pulling the shawl of her kurta tighter around her neck, where a blue-black bruise was just beginning to form, spreading slowly like a pool of spilled ink.

He took his first sip and She felt giddy, whether with muted euphoria or crushing melancholy She couldn't tell. Then the second, then the third, and finally He slumped back, drooling from the corner of his mouth, his glass forgotten on the arm of the chair.

She wasn't surprised when He started to talk. She had expected it, expected his voice to spill out of now-white lips that didn't even move.

'Remember when we first saw each other.'

It wasn't a question and She didn't reply.

'You were wearing a pink kurta and your hair was much

longer then. I don't know what you thought of me. Probably nothing good. I was balding, short and had quite a stomach. But there you were, all sweet and quiet, sitting between your mother and your father, not even looking at me, playing the part of the shy, good girl. You didn't say anything. Your parents and my parents talked. I looked at you and thought, what a world. A girl like you for a guy like me.'

He hadn't spoken to her like this in years. Not since that long, long stay in the hospital. The years since then had been stony silence in the morning, crippling loneliness during the day and desperate paranoia at night. There was no time for talk. He spoke to his friends and She spoke to the vegetable vendor, the trash collector, the cold store lady.

But now here She was, listening to him say things She wished He had when He was able. She looked at the television blankly, not registering the fast-moving images. The television belted laughter and talk but in her mind was a steadily building buzz, a cacophony of crickets rising in a crescendo. His voice, a monotone and vacuous, cut through the buzz like a cleaver, coming in strong and clear.

'Do you remember how scared you were when we went boating in Fewa Tal? I hated boats but I only took you because you said you had never been in the middle of the lake. You were so afraid, grabbing my hand and almost tipping the boat over. I don't think I could've saved you if we had fallen over. You blushed each time you held my hand because you were so naïve. Never had a boyfriend even.'

She remembered. He had worn sunglasses too big for his face and had the top button of his shirt undone. He had rowed fast and hard, their boat cutting smoothly through the water like a knife. Once out in the middle of the lake, the water turned a deep greyish-green. A gently rocking boat floating on peerless depths. She had looked into the darkness and, in it, found only her creased reflection. As if ravaged by time, her crumpled face rippled in the water and She felt as if something unbearably heavy had been suddenly placed upon her shoulders. She was afraid for the first of countless times.

She had been so young then, barely out of college. One by one all of her friends and cousins had gotten married and She was the youngest single girl. There hadn't been much outright pressure from her family. They were educated people who would never have forced their daughter into a marriage She didn't want. In the end, it was her choice. She felt it was time and told her parents to find someone. She had never had a boyfriend before, always too shy to approach anyone herself and always seen as too standoffish to be approached. She wasn't ugly but She wasn't beautiful either. Her girlfriends considered her homely while the boys considered her plain. She was forgettable, and if She hadn't been at the top of her class, no one would've noticed her.

She didn't pick him, He picked her. She just agreed. He didn't seem better or worse than any of the other boys who had come to see her. In their very first meeting alone, He was gregarious and charming and He made her laugh. They saw each other on and off for six months while their parents worked out all the wedding nitty-gritty. There were saris to be bought and blouses to be sewn, jewellery to be designed, precious stones to be set and gold to be fashioned. She didn't mind that He was balding, had a paunch and was at least five years older than her. He was funny and smart and He kept her entertained whenever they went out. She liked the way He started to casually hold her hand after their second date and how He made no moves to kiss her until after their wedding. She wouldn't have minded even if He had tried during their courtship, but She appreciated the restraint.

But all that seemed so long ago, and now those times existed only in between the pages of a photo album and in the dark recesses of her own mind. Now, here they were, out of space and out of time, and all that She kept hidden under the covers threatened to come bursting out. She looked at him and saw surprise. His eyes were wide against the tan leather of his Bahun face, with its large aquiline nose, thick dark eyebrows and the saggy, fleshy cheeks of a heavy drinker.

She remembered their honeymoon. They had stayed in Pokhara for a week and He had never wanted to leave the hotel room. She recalled that week clearly and immutably in time, as the sweep of memory now hurled towards her like a hurricane. The hotel room had smelled musty and dank. The large single bed had confused her, with its many sheets and blankets tucked in tight. That first night had been terribly painful, She had cried into his shoulder but He hadn't seemed to notice. The times after weren't so bad, she concentrated on the sounds of the streets, the birds and the lake and it was soon over. It wasn't that He was a selfish lover. He didn't know what He was doing and She didn't know what She wanted.

It was on the third day. She had left to go the store while

He slept. She was carrying and sipping from a bottle of water on her return, when it slithered out of her hands and spilled onto the bed next to where He slept, a dark stain spreading across the clean white linen. He had risen slowly and slapped her easily—as though the act were an affectation, a habit. She had held her stinging cheek, stymied by shock. Outside, the lake gleamed like a mirror and there were birds calling. The sun was high and the mountains looked frighteningly blue and frighteningly close. Later, when it was night and He slipped into bed, She wept like a child. He cradled her head in his arms, saying it would be okay. Never even an apology.

'I always loved you, you know,' He said.

This genuinely surprised her. This She had not expected. The words fell like pots and pans, clanging like the riot they made when She clamoured to escape his roving palms. She didn't know love, especially not from him.

'I never loved you like I loved you in the hospital. You were sitting on that hospital bed, your gown had fallen open at your thighs and you hadn't even bothered to close it. You weren't crying but your eyes looked like my father's did when he died. I sat next to you and held you in my arms and you cried. I had never felt so close before.'

She remembered the hospital too. The dirty, spit-stained walls, the mass of humanity lining the emergency room, the red-eyed mothers and the smoking fathers. Her hospital gown was green and so were the curtains around her. That was after the blood and there had been so much blood. She had fainted and come to and fainted again. She felt torn, a long cherished part of her ripped and dead.

That long episode in the hospital had taken something from her and He knew it very well. For the first twenty-four hours She was almost catatonic, refusing or unable to speak, only blinking. When they got back from the hospital, He had bought her a Labrador puppy—Kanchi, a tiny, brown ball of a thing. Looking at the puppy as it tried to gnaw on the toona of her dressing gown She felt a twinge of the love that had so cruelly been denied to her.

She loved that dog like a daughter and Kanchi too seemed to sense just how much her presence meant to the household. Wherever She went Kanchi followed, not that She left the house much. But whether she was cooking in the kitchen, gardening in their tiny yard or washing clothes on the sunny roof, Kanchi was never far off, resting her head on her two paws, one eye always open. Anytime She felt inconsolable, anytime She woke from uneasy dreams with a sweaty brow, anytime She collapsed on her bed from sheer emotional exhaustion, Kanchi was always around to nudge her with her wet nose, a sock in her mouth and her tail wagging. And while Kanchi was around, He never so much as raised his hand. Once when He had grabbed her hard by the wrist and pulled, Kanchi had almost taken a chunk out of his calf.

'You cried so much when that car hit Kanchi,' He continued. Even now, thinking about that day made her want to vomit. Try as She might, She couldn't erase the image of Kanchi crushed under the wheel of his friend's Maruti. She had cried and cried then, but so had He. It was the first time and last time She would see him cry over anything.

After the hospital, after Kanchi, She had hoped it would

stop. But these things never do. Her cheek burned often from the force of his fingers. Anything was a provocation. It wasn't that he was a violent man, he rarely raised his voice at her or others. He preferred to resolve differences with a smart joke and a pat on the back. She had seen him speak to the neighbour when Kanchi had fertilized their compound one too many times. The neighbour, Acharya uncle, had been fuming, but He cracked a joke about *Kartik-lagya kukkur haru* and the two were soon talking politics, Kanchi and her antics forgotten. It was only with her that He felt comfortable.

She walked as if in a minefield, her heart always in her throat and a stifled scream on her tongue. She recalled clearly the purple welts on her inner thighs, the deep crimson of the blood when his knuckles broke skin, the stabbing of a thousand knives each time She breathed in from when He cracked a rib. Through the thousands, She remembered them all, filed away in the deep, animal part of her brain that is all instinct and all vengeance.

'Do you remember what I said to you in the hospital that day? There's no going back now. You know why I said that? Because you are my wife. I thought of leaving you but I couldn't. I loved you. You needed me as much as I needed you. But there was just no going back for me.'

There was really no going back for her either. Maybe if She was serious about divorce, her parents would have come around to it. They were, after all, educated people. But Kathmandu is no city for a widow. Moreover, it wasn't that She hated him always.

A snatch of song, from somewhere in the neighbourhood

or somewhere in the mind, came to the fore. A muted melody, faint and unrecognizable.

'Remember those songs I used to sing for you?'

There were a few. Old Hindi songs mostly, Dev Anand prancing around with a damsel. He played the guitar comfortably, at ease with the instrument. He played easily and sang comfortably, his voice resonating. He sang to her, often on his knees and looking directly into her eyes. His birthday gift to her every year was a song, written and composed while at work. He would bring flowers, an ornate, sugary cake and sing to her while She laughed and laughed.

'I hope you will forgive me, but even if you don't, I'm still sorry. I would like to think that you loved me once, even if you don't anymore. I was never very good at showing you just how much I loved you. I tried but I always felt like I never did enough, like I wasn't a good enough husband. You were always the perfect wife. You never complained, you did what I asked and we got along perfectly. We didn't even have to talk. No one understood me like you did.'

She felt a manic urge to laugh but She held it back. If let loose, the laughter would turn into hysterics and then into mania. She didn't want to go crazy, at least not yet.

Their second and final trip abroad had been to Darjeeling on a holiday. For three days in the hills She was in love. This was the honeymoon they had never really had. Away from the deep, placid water that hid unknowable depths, the rolling open hills were a comfort. On their last evening there they sat on the grass and looked out at the lights coming on inside houses as dusk fell. She leaned against him and, in the half light, He kissed her.

She stood and walked over to his chair, where his body was already beginning to slide towards the floor, stiff as a wooden plank. She sat rigidly on the edge of the chair and pulled him up, wiping away the drool with the edge of her shawl and closing his cavernous eyes. She put her arms around him and listened for his heartbeat.

'I'm sorry,' He said into her hair.

'It's okay,' She whispered back.

She cradled his head to her chest and looked down at his scalp—the errant strands of hair surrounding a gleaming skull, the flakes of peeling skin. In that lost moment, She pitied him. This weak man, this broken man.

It hadn't taken much thinking for her to come to her decision. There was nothing immediate, no casus belli. Years can numb discomfort, but sometimes you find it starts to rankle. Like coming across a wound you had forgotten about. It hadn't been the baby, He had had nothing to do with that. He actually took scrupulous care to avoid her swelling belly. It hadn't been Kanchi, who was the largest hole in her being. It was everything that wearied her and brought her down, as if a millstone were hanging around her neck. This, perhaps, was what they meant by quiet desperation. And, one day, while cleaning the dishes, she had come to a conclusion. They had been having a rat problem and an opened bottle of Royal Stag was always around.

She kissed the top of his head, a gesture He would never have allowed. She stood and wandered aimlessly through the house, opening closed windows and closing open ones. When She made her way back to the living room, He was in the same position She had left him, only his eyes had opened again. She looked into them and into the empty black void of his pupils. She found only herself looking back. She thought back to that time on the water but this time, the reflection was of herself as She was, still young, her eyes large, her nose small. She felt herself being carried, like a boat on a lake, borne by the currents of time.

The Red Kurta

Sharmila came into the Thapa household at the age of twelve. Her uncle, Mohan, brought her to Kathmandu, an eighteen-hour bus ride on which Sharmila vomited copiously into a plastic bag. Multiple times. It was the turns, she would explain later. Sharmila didn't remember much of that bus ride, but she recalled clearly the jolting tempo ride into the heart of Kathmandu. 'Lazimpat!' the conductor had shouted, jolting her further. To Sharmila the Thapa house was palatial, maybe what the king's palace looked like. The marble porch gleamed and Sharmila slid playfully on its smooth surface while waiting outside for the Thapas. Rani, the matriarch, gave her a chocolate as a welcome gift.

I was visiting that day and happened to catch Sharmila's arrival. She was just a child, wide-eyed and sleek of hair. As she passed me on the way into the house, I caught a whiff of stale vomit. We sat down in the Thapas' living room, with Rani seated in a regal purple armchair and Sharmila, the supplicant, cross-legged on the floor. She didn't talk much, only played absently with her hair. Mohan and Rani negotiated.

Mohan then took Sharmila aside and talked to her for long about all that was going to happen. She didn't seem to understand much but nodded along. A magnificent new house, nice new people and the city of Kathmandu for the first time! What young village girl would've refused? Mohan left her with five hundred rupees, more money than she had ever had before. That night Sharmila would lie for the first time on a soft cushioned mattress in her own room, under blankets that smelled like rain and pillows that felt like wool. She would fall asleep to the taste of sweet rich milk chocolate, the kind she'd never even dreamt of before.

Sharmila's second and third days were uneventful. Later she would describe how easily the first few days merged with the thousands that came after. After that initial burst of happiness, everything seemed to blur into one single day, endlessly repeating itself. She would wake every day at 6 a.m. and help make breakfast for the family. There would be eggs to crack, beat and sprinkle with salt. She'd put bread in the toaster, two by two, jumping with fright the first time the brown toast popped out. There would be juice in one glass and tea in all the others. This she was taught by Rani, a sharp, biting smack on her arm each time she forgot something. It wasn't too painful. Only humiliating.

Sharmila would first serve breakfast to Kumar, the only Thapa child. Even though he was the same age as Sharmila, Rani asked her to call him dai. Kumar didn't take very well to Sharmila. It took him some time to get used to ordering her around, though, to be fair, it didn't take him long to learn. 'Sharmila!' he would scream for her, and keep up the screaming until she came running. Then, lounging on his bed and watching television, he would ask for a glass of water or maybe a snack. He was never cruel to her, like Raja and Rani sometimes were, just demanding. He never hit or reprimanded her. If he was angry, he would simply stare at her and keep staring until she left the room or did what he wanted her to. During these times Sharmila always tried very hard to avoid his eyes, but even then she found herself searching them out, as if only to reassure herself that they were still there.

Sharmila and Kumar grew up together. Raja and Rani didn't seem to take too well to the fact that their son's only friend, or rather acquaintance, was the servant girl. Kumar was a shy boy, never the rambunctious type, always with his head in a book or in the clouds. But by the time Sharmila's first year at the Thapas came to a close, the two had become fast friends. On many occasions, I'd spy the two of them involved in some elaborate play-acting out in the Thapas' ample lawn. And Kumar's first question, whenever he got home from school, was always, Sharmila khoi?

Sharmila kept a strict timetable. At 4.30 p.m. she would finish up washing the dishes from lunch and start preparing tea. When Kumar got back, she would serve him juice and a snack and tea to the adults. By 6 p.m., once done with tea, she would sneak into Kumar's room where he would be watching TV. Sharmila was fascinated by the television. Back home there was only a single television. Every Saturday, half the village gathered outside Gurungba's house to watch the weekly 2 p.m. Bollywood movie on Nepal TV. At the Thapas', there was always something on. Kumar almost never watched Nepali shows or even Hindi shows. He liked cartoons in English. Sharmila couldn't understand what was being said, she could barely even read Nepali, having dropped out of school in Class 3 to help around the house. She liked to look at the pictures, the animals and the funny people. Whenever Kumar laughed at something, Sharmila would smile too, as if she got the joke.

Midway through Sharmila's second year at the Thapas', Kumar started to teach Sharmila English. Whenever I came over for dinner, I would watch the two of them in the living room, bent over exercise books. For an hour every evening, Kumar made Sharmila write out the alphabets from A to Z. In that hour no one was allowed to ask anything of Sharmila. Kumar refused to allow Sharmila out of his sight until she had copied down the alphabet—which he laid out neatly at the top of the exercise book—in her scraggly disjointed handwriting. By the end of the year Sharmila could read very basic English and say a few words. She couldn't understand the television, they spoke too fast she said, but she could read some of the signs. Whenever she recognized a word, she would say it out loud, slowly, enunciating each syllable. At times like these, Kumar would beam at her, visibly happy.

The Thapas didn't seem to mind this indulgence Kumar was showing the girl. They were proud of the fact that Kumar had taken such an interest in helping those less fortunate, a fact they announced at every party and to anyone who would listen. At the bank where we worked, Ajay, or 'Raja' as Sharmila was supposed to call him, could not stop repeating just how kind-hearted and good-intentioned his only son Kumar was.

I never thought of Ajay as a bad man. He was quiet, wore glasses and didn't gossip or flirt. He was a good family man, always trying to keep his wife and son content. Sometimes he would burst into their home and announce that the entire family would be going out to dinner. They'd tell Sharmila to eat the rice and vegetables left over from lunch while they went out. Sometimes there were no leftovers, and Sharmila would take the opportunity to steal two slices of bread, butter one side, jam on the other and eat them with some tea. She knew Rani would clip her ears if she ever found out so Sharmila took pains to wash all the utensils she used till they were spotless and smooth. When she ate, she relished the forbidden taste.

Speaking of Rani, now, there was a woman. Rani was the kind of woman every man thinks he wants, not realizing that a girl like her would never want a man who would want someone like her. Rani had short, close-cropped dark hair that she pared into a Thai cut. Her eyes, when naked, sparkled with energy, but often, at night, they would be obscured by square glasses with thick black frames. She almost always wore pants, tight butt-hugging jeans that showed off her figure. Rani didn't work. She came from money so she invested cash here and there, went to charity events and drank mimosas in the sun with her expatriate friends.

Little by little Sharmila got to know both the Thapa parents. She knew that Raja liked his tea darker than most others. She knew he liked the colour blue and almost always wore blue shirts to work. She knew that Rani liked to go for a jog first thing in the morning, and so always placed a fresh towel near the entrance in anticipation. She knew that, in the winter, they both liked their own hot water bottles to cuddle with.

From what I could fathom, it wasn't that the Thapas were cruel. They treated Sharmila kindly, just not equally. In their minds they were treating her better than most others treated their servants. Sharmila had her own room and her own bathroom. Rani bought her clothes once or twice a year and they always gave her enough to eat. Of course, what they fed her was never what they ate themselves. While their breakfast consisted of eggs, toast, juice and sausages, Sharmila's was always two slices of plain white bread with a cup of tea. When Raja brought home momos for dinner, Sharmila ate leftovers. Once Rani caught her sneaking a momo while they were being heated and slapped her hard across the face, yelling, 'Just ask!'

But Sharmila could never ask, especially not for food. She had once asked Raja for a piece of chocolate that he was giving to Kumar and Raja had looked at her amazed. Eyes wide, he said, 'This is Swiss chocolate.'

By the end of Sharmila's second year, she had mastered all her work around the house. She could cook just as well as Rani, which wasn't saying much as Rani could barely cook. The woman who used to do the cooking before Sharmila came along was a squat figure, barely able to reach the cupboards. She consistently used too much salt and there was always too much grease. I once complimented Sharmila on her chicken gravy and she blushed, leaving quickly and saying nothing.

Sharmila made breakfast for the whole family, and cooked lunch and dinner while Rani acted like she helped. She had learned to operate the vacuum cleaner on her own and was also able to turn on the television and change channels. By herself she had also mastered basic addition and subtraction through the trips she made to the local stores. All the while she still learnt English from Kumar.

Sharmila went home once a year, during Dashain. Raja paid her salary then and Rani usually bought her a new kurta-suruwal. Always before she left, Raja and Rani took pains to be exceedingly nice to her. By the time she was fourteen, Sharmila had figured out why. We'll miss you, they'd say. Rani would stroke Sharmila's hair while Raja would smile magnanimously. Only Kumar would be in his room, refusing to come out. He was the only one who seemed to genuinely miss her, and not just her labour, she would say later. But Sharmila went home, buying sweets and bangles for her sisters along the way and depositing the rest of her pay with her father. Sharmila's father, Krishna, didn't like the fact that his daughter was working in the city. But he didn't make enough as a bricklayer and needed his two younger daughters around to take care of the house. Sharmila's income was what carried them through the year as Krishna usually blew his earnings fast. He didn't drink like the others did but he was kind and there are always those who will take advantage of a good heart. When Dashain ended, like always, Sharmila returned to the Thapas. She knew little else.

By the end of Sharmila's third year, Kumar and Sharmila had both turned fifteen. Kumar was growing at an alarming rate, already a head taller than his father. His limbs were long and gangly, his body thin and lean. He still abhorred physical activity and spent most of his time in his room, the door locked and music blasting. Sharmila could never understand the words to the songs and the music itself sounded violent and angry. Kumar didn't watch much television anymore and even their English lessons gradually stopped. Whenever Sharmila attempted to enter Kumar's room, the door was always locked.

While Kumar was growing, so was Sharmila. And Sharmila was beautiful. Had she been given the kind of conditioning Rani had when growing up, Sharmila would have easily outclassed her. Even in her dirty yellow kurta, she was radiant. Her hair was long and braided, hanging down to her waist, and her hands, despite being calloused and cracked from work and washing dishes, had slim feminine fingers that worked deftly and with skill. Kumar noticed, I'm certain. He noticed her hands as she flipped an omelette, her fingers long but the nails always short and clean. He noticed how fresh her hair smelled. I watched as he watched her move across the room, always elegant, never clumsy, never stumbling. He noticed her eyes and, for a change, it was he who sought hers out.

But others noticed too. Raja and I once arrived to melodrama. Rani was standing defiantly in the doorway, her legs apart and her hands on her hips. Inside, Sharmila was on the floor, sobbing quietly. 'Ask her what happened,' Rani said immediately when she saw us. 'Ask her.'

I knelt beside Sharmila and asked her, 'Sharmila, *ke bhayo?*'

Before another sob could escape Sharmila's throat, Rani had already stepped in. 'This uttauli. I was coming back from the store and you know what I saw? She was with that security guard from next door and he had his hands inside her shirt!'

'What?' Raja was incredulous. He turned to Sharmila, 'Did you let him do this?'

In between chest hitches, Sharmila mumbled a no. I believed her. I had seen the security guard leering at Rani's behind more than a couple of times. If anyone was to blame here, it must have been him.

'What else did you let him do?' Rani thundered.

Sharmila just kept crying and I felt it best to leave just then. But I asked Sharmila about that night later and she was frank about it. The guard had forcefully put his hands under her kurta, even though she had protested and tried to get away. But Sharmila didn't wear a bra; she tied a rectangle of cloth tight across her breasts, which the guard hadn't been able to penetrate. I asked her if the cloth didn't hurt and she said, yes, of course, as if that were the most natural thing in the world.

It was Kumar's sixteenth birthday. There were close to fifty people in the house. Raja was magnanimously pouring drinks for everyone, despite having hired a bartender for the night. Sharmila was weaving through the guests with a plate of canapés. She was wearing a new kurta, one that I hadn't seen her in before, a deep red with a pattern of ornate blue flowers over the left side. The flowers were set with tiny mirrors and they reflected back the light like a million eyes. Her hair was pulled back tight in a long ponytail and there was gajal around her eyes. A constant smile played on her lips, even as she balanced plates while nimbly dodging wobbly drunkards.

Rani called for the cake and everyone wandered into the

dining room. I was in the kitchen getting a drink when Sharmila sauntered in, a tray of glasses and dirty dishes on her hands. There was another person in the room besides us, Raghav, Raja's cousin, in a loud floral tie. Sharmila bent slightly to deposit the dishes into the sink and Raghav leaned forward, reached out one unsteady hand and grabbed a fistful of her butt-cheek. Sharmila jerked upright but continued depositing glasses as if nothing had happened. Oblivious to my presence, Raghav slurred, 'I really like bhotini girls,' before exiting. I followed him out but my mind was elsewhere. I couldn't seem to get the image of Raghav's hand on Sharmila's behind out of my mind.

Outside, the birthday party was a success. The men were happy and drunk, the women angry and drunk. I was the last to leave so Rani wanted Kumar to come down and say goodbye. She yelled up at him, 'Kumar! Kumar!' When close to five minutes had passed and Kumar still didn't appear, Rani walked up smartly to his room, her heels clacking on the marble. She knocked on the door, loudly and insistently. There was music from within, muted, so Rani turned the handle and the door opened. There was a half-scream, stifled with her hand.

Kumar was sitting up on his bed with Sharmila standing off to the side, hands clasped in front and head down. Kumar stared defiantly at his mother.

'Her head was on his lap,' Rani said. 'Her head was on his lap,' she said again, as if saying it twice would make it untrue. And she was holding his hand,' Rani muttered, under her breath.

'What?' said Raja. I don't know whether he really hadn't heard or if he just couldn't believe his ears.

Rani stomped across the room and grabbed Sharmila by the shoulders, beginning to shake her. 'Don't you dare touch my son, you whore,' she spat. 'Don't you dare, don't you dare, don't you dare.' It was the first time I'd seen Rani in that way, lips curled in a snarl, her face a hate-mask. I couldn't help but think of just how unattractive she was right then.

Sharmila started to cry and Rani released her. Sharmila slid to the ground, sobbing furiously while Rani stood over her like a wrathful demoness. Rani made a visible effort to calm down, taking a deep breath and speaking through her teeth, 'I want every dish washed before you sleep tonight. You don't get to eat.'

Sharmila stood and quietly left. Rani stared at Kumar for a while. Kumar looked back. Getting no answer, she stormed off, slamming the door behind her. Raja glanced awkwardly at me and then followed his wife out. I took this opportunity to make my own exit, quickly and quietly.

This was how Sharmila described the first time she learned. Rani didn't speak to Sharmila all morning, only gestured and gave terse commands. Rani was usually chirpy in the morning, sipping coffee and supervising Sharmila. After Raja left, she retired to her room, put on her make-up, and made sure her hair was perfect. Sharmila waited impatiently for Rani to leave so that she could have the house all to herself and not have to endure Rani's reproachful gaze, but Rani simply sat on the leather sofa, idly flipping channels.

It was past 1 p.m. when a short, nervous but strikingly handsome man arrived at the door. Sharmila had never seen him before. He had a thin moustache and swung his briefcase before him like a weapon. When Sharmila opened the door, the man surveyed her thoroughly, looking her over from top to bottom. Sharmila felt consumed in his glance, as if he had opened his mouth wide and swallowed her whole. Rani met him in the hallway and beckoned to Sharmila while the man flopped casually into an easy chair and placed his briefcase by his feet. Rani handed Sharmila some money and rattled off a list of groceries and sundries to buy. She departed hurriedly, afraid she would forget something essential.

Outside the gate of the Thapa home, Sharmila was accosted again by the security guards who worked for the manpower company next door. There were two of them now, swarthy and unshaven, smelling of sweat and cheap mustard hair oil. With a coy smile, she managed to evade them both and finish her shopping. On her return, they were waiting for her. Hidden in the Thapas' driveway, they pounced the moment she appeared in view. They didn't grab her, simply barred her way.

'Ke cha ta, soltini?' one said.

Sharmila tried to sidle past but one of them grabbed her hand as she passed. His palm, big and sweaty, felt like an animal on her skin. There was a look in their eyes that reminded Sharmila of pigs and mad cows. The other placed his hand on her left breast and kneaded it hard through the flimsy cloth of her kurta, hurting her. Sharmila struggled and managed to get past. She ran to the house, lugging her bag of groceries. At the entrance, a few tomatoes spilled out and Sharmila spent a full ten minutes finding them and stuffing them back into the bag, her legs and hands shaking uncontrollably. Over at the gate, the security guards stood laughing.

When Sharmila presented the groceries to Rani, she was sitting on her bed alone, brushing her hair. The handsome man had left. From among the sundries, Rani picked out a bar of bathing soap, a bottle of shampoo and a wide-tooth comb and handed them to Sharmila, smiling.

'For you,' she said.

At first Sharmila stood dumbfounded, but then accepted the gifts gratefully. She left quickly, before Rani could change her mind. In the sanctuary of her room, Sharmila peeled the plastic wrapper from the comb and unfurled her thick hair that had grown long and tangled. Carefully, she threaded the comb through her locks and brushed gently but insistently, savouring the pleasure of having her tangles come out. While Sharmila brushed contentedly, the room seemed to shrink around her. What had once seemed so very big and lavish now seemed smaller than Kumar's closet. The pillows were flat and smelled a little while the blankets were frayed, with the stuffing showing. There was a strong smell of rat droppings, a sour musty odour that seemed to have not a single source but was all-pervasive.

After that, Rani seemed to have all but forgotten the incident with Kumar. She regularly sent Sharmila out on errands, bought her essentials and even gave her extra food, speaking softly and smiling often. Raja too displayed no ill-will and treated Sharmila as he always had. Kumar, on the other hand, seemed more distant than usual.

When the moustachioed man visited the Thapa household again, Sharmila was busy sweeping the floor. Bent over and intent on dislodging a particularly stubborn dust bunny from under the refrigerator, she didn't even notice the man enter the house. He didn't knock or ring the doorbell, simply strode in confidently, swinging his briefcase. It was only when she felt a caress on the small of her back that Sharmila jerked upright, suddenly aware. The man looked her up and down again, as if evaluating her. A smile played on his lips, as if he was satisfied with what he surveyed. Sharmila self-consciously clutched the front of her kurta, demure under his naked gaze.

The man left, saying nothing, and Sharmila found herself in Kumar's room. He was sitting on the bed, reading a book. There was music playing, a strange, disconcerting jangling that Sharmila found abrasive but which reminded her of wide open plains at night, thunder and lightning and dark things. He's old and his skin is cold, Sharmila recalled the words to me. She told Kumar of what had just happened, the words stumbling awkwardly from her mouth. Then she found herself telling Kumar about the security guards. Kumar asked a lot of questions.

'Did it feel good?' he asked again and again, as if excited. 'Where did he touch you? Did he kiss you? Did it feel good? Did it feel good?'

The next day, Raja and Rani had an argument over breakfast. Raja asked why Shishir visited her so often.

'He doesn't,' Rani replied shortly.

'What do you talk about?'

'Business.'

'You don't have any business!' Raja exploded unexpectedly, his glasses comically askew and his newspaper tossed to the floor.

'You don't know anything, Ajay,' Rani said, still avoiding his eyes. 'Don't bring this up in front of Kumar.'

'I want to know what's going on,' said Kumar calmly.

'No!' Rani said, reflexively.

Raja slowly removed his glasses, took a deep breath and began to rub his temples vigorously. Then he put his glasses back on and abruptly rose from the table. He got in his car and went to work. After 5 p.m., he came home with me. It seems Raja didn't really have any friends.

Sharmila, standing in the kitchen and listening to Raja and Rani argue, understood what was happening. But before she could process it, she was seized with nausea. The very thought of Rani with that man, that disgusting man who'd run his fingers down her back! She ran to the kitchen and vomited into the sink, heave after heave.

That night, Raja explained to me how Shishir was an old friend of Rani's. The two of them had gone to college in India together where he'd always suspected they'd been lovers. He'd gotten it out of Sharmila that a mustachioed man visited every few days. He knew then it was Shishir and that their marriage was over.

Back home Sharmila couldn't sleep, there was a queasiness in her stomach and yet she felt a strange hunger. She quietly tiptoed to Kumar's room and pushed the door open. She closed the door behind her and slowly turned the lock. Kumar was in bed but stood up and embraced her. He stroked her hair and her face, and she buried her face in his chest.

'Please?' asked Kumar.

'Nai,' Sharmila protested.

'Please,' Kumar pleaded mournfully. 'Everyone does it.'

'I don't like it,' Sharmila protested again.

'It makes me happy,' Kumar said.

And so she did.

Raja left my place early the next day. He said he wanted to eat breakfast with his son. Rani grudgingly emerged from her room and sat at the breakfast table, sipping tea from a Formica cup. Kumar barely said a word as he ate. He only looked up at Sharmila constantly.

Sharmila felt queasy again, just like she had the day before. She ran to the kitchen to vomit and was bent over the sink ejecting a liquid stream onto dirty cups half-filled with tea when Rani grabbed her arm from behind and twisted her around.

'Are you sick?' she asked, her face inches from Sharmila's, which reeked of bile.

'No,' Sharmila replied, confused.

'Then why are you vomiting?'

'Khoi…' said Sharmila. 'I don't know.'

Rani dragged Sharmila by the arm to her room.

'What are you up to?' she muttered to herself, rifling through Sharmila's clothes and the few belongings she had.

Underneath a towel, Rani found a red kurta, a fine cotton piece, inlaid with dainty blue flowers. She held it up in her hands, scrutinizing it. There was a dark red stain near the lower hem of the kurta, the red here darker than anywhere else.

'I didn't buy you that,' said Rani. 'Where did you get this from?'

'I…I bought it myself,' said Sharmila, not meeting Rani's gaze.

'Don't lie to me,' Rani sprang forward, clawing at Sharmila's cheeks. 'Where did you get it from?' Sharmila shrank to a corner and made a strangled sound, as if something were caught in her throat.

'Where?' Rani asked again.

Sharmila said nothing.

'Why are you vomiting all the time?' Rani asked slowly.

Sharmila said nothing.

Rani was still going through her things while Raja and Kumar watched from the doorway. She fished out a bag of clothes from beneath the bed and upended it. Four dark Nepali topis, a brown wool muffler and an old tweed coat tumbled out.

'You stole these?' Rani was livid. 'These are Raja's.' Her pale hands were shaking with rage.

Raja walked over, picked up the coat and fingered it, as if he couldn't believe it was his old coat from his own closet.

'I've never even seen you wear those,' said Kumar dryly from the doorway. He was standing rigidly and staring at both his parents.

'It doesn't matter. She stole,' Rani replied harshly, biting down on the words as if chopping each syllable in two. 'Are they for your lover?' Rani took a few threatening steps towards Sharmila, who shrunk even deeper into her corner.

'They're for baba,' Sharmila whispered, afraid of the woman looming over her.

Rani snatched up the clothes and stomped out. Raja followed her out while Kumar leaned against the doorframe for a while, hands deep in his pockets, his head bowed. He tried to meet Sharmila's eyes but she didn't seem to want to look at him. He, too, left.

Sharmila closed the door and locked it firmly behind the departing Thapas. She collapsed on her bed, on top of all her clothes. She cried openly and loudly, tears soaking through and leaving dark splotches on the fabric underneath. Her cries rebounded off the walls and came back to her amplified. After she grew tired of hearing herself, she looked for her kurta, the red one. She inspected it closely for any tears that the overzealous Rani might have made and, finding none, she put it on. She looked at herself in the small hand mirror hanging on her door by a nail. She stretched this way and that, trying to get a good, complete look in the tiny frame. She ran a hand down the front, smoothing out the creases and let loose her hair from its tight braid. She looked at her face in the glass, framed by her ink-black hair like a halo. She looked into her eyes, large and brown, always expressive, but now red-rimmed. Her cheeks were flushed, her skin darker and fuller. Sharmila was not like the women on television whose flawless glowing skin and perfectly styled hair brought forth in her an unquenchable envy. She knew she could never compete with them. But she often saw young Kathmandu girls in the street, riding on scooters and walking hand-in-hand with their boyfriends and wondered if her own conservative kurta with her tight cloth-bra didn't seem better than their ass-high shorts, their loose T-shirts and tight dresses that always seemed to be revealing everything. She felt that she had something that these girls had lost.

Sharmila had taken off the kurta, folded it carefully and gingerly, and placed it under her mattress when Rani attempted to barge into Sharmila's room. She kicked the door until Sharmila unlocked it. Rani curtly handed Sharmila a long, cylindrical pen-like object and ordered her to take it into the toilet and piss on it. Sharmila stood there with the pregnancy test in her hand, uncomprehending. Rani repeated herself, slowly, enunciating every word as if she were speaking to a child. Sharmila did as she was asked.

Rani held the test gingerly with a tissue, shaking it vigorously. Sharmila sat on her bed, still not comprehending what was happening.

'You're pregnant,' Rani announced grimly.

Sharmila felt as if she was sliding to the floor even though she remained sitting. She heard Rani's words as if from a great distance and they seemed to echo on and on in her mind. She knew what pregnancy was and she knew what it implied. After all, she'd seen those Nepali films where the heroine is raped and gives birth to a bastard. It was as if gravity had increased, pulling her as if she were an iron filing drawn by a magnet to the floor.

'Whose is it?' Rani asked, her voice low and dangerous. Raja had appeared beside Rani and they stood together, reconciled in the face of such an affront to their propriety. Everything else was forgotten, or rather sublimated and deflected, like a bullet, at Sharmila.

'Who did you sleep with?' Rani asked again, getting no response from Sharmila.

'Was it in my house?' Raja spoke from beside Rani, his arm now around her waist, both supporting her and drawing anger from her.

'Tell me who!' Rani yelled and took a step forward, raising her hand. Sharmila closed her eyes and waited for the sting to subside. A red palm was outlined on her cheek.

Kumar was now at the door, standing beside his parents. Sharmila looked to him, searching for his eyes. They were vacant and vacuous, seeing her but not quite.

Rani had had enough of the charade. She hauled Sharmila up bodily by her hair. Fingers digging deep into her scalp, she dragged Sharmila out. All the while Sharmila didn't make so much as a whimper.

'Who gave you that kurta?' she asked incessantly as she dragged her. 'Was it your lover? What have you done in my house you randi?'

'She was wearing it on my birthday,' Sharmila heard Kumar say dreamily from behind them but no one paid him any attention. They were too invested in the spectacle of kicking out the whore.

Rani threw Sharmila outside the gate and Raja brought along a plastic bag of Sharmila's clothes which he

unceremoniously dumped on the ground. He threw three
hundred rupees from his wallet at her.

'You probably get more than that from your customer,'
Rani spat. 'This is what happens when you treat them well.
They begin to step on your head.'

Sharmila slowly gathered her clothes and stuffed the money
into her bra. She looked at the Thapas, that happy family of
three. Raja and Rani stood next to each other, as if barring her
way back in. Kumar stood off to one side, gazing stonily at
her.

'Kumar,' she started to say.

'Don't you dare,' Rani threatened, again raising her open
palm.

They turned and walked away. Kumar lingered, as if he
wanted to say something. He stared at Sharmila stuffing
clothes into her plastic bag as if in a daze. Finally, he shook his
head and followed his parents. Inside the gate, he turned and
firmly locked the door.

I found Sharmila sitting outside the Thapas' gate the next day
when I came over. It was a Saturday and I was supposed to
pick up Raja and Rani for an office party. One of our tellers
was getting married. I had raised my hand to press the bell
when I saw her curled on the concrete next to the gate, her
head on some clothes, her kurta dirty and stained. I spoke her
name and she woke, groggy. She started to cry before I could
say anything. After she'd explained what had happened, I

took her home to my flat. The wedding was forgotten. What else could I have done? Raja and Rani were my friends but this way no way to treat someone.

Sharmila didn't mention the pregnancy until later. 'It wasn't hard to fall in love with him,' she said. 'He paid attention to me, never raised his voice and always brought me things. Sometimes chocolates, other times two samosas wrapped in a newspaper, and once, even a new red kurta. I knew he was always following me with his eyes.'

She explained how she would feel his eyes travel up and down her body, raising goosebumps. When he talked to her, he looked defiantly into her eyes, as if daring her to look back. She did, once, and thought she would go blind. She only just glanced at his eyes, like the brusque brush of two sets of lips, and looked away, down, here, there, anywhere except. Sometimes he touched her, a hand on an arm or even the gentle brush of his hips as he passed and she would shudder involuntarily, even when just thinking of these moments when alone in her room. 'It just was so easy to love him,' she said.

'He was taking advantage of you,' I tried to explain.

She looked up at me and something of a smile played on her face. 'He loves me too,' she said. 'I know that.'

Sharmila stayed with me for a few days, waiting for her father to come pick her up. In all her years in Kathmandu, she had never been allowed farther away than the grocery store. When the Thapas kicked her out, she had nowhere to go. I would come home from work to find her standing at the window, staring out at the cars and bikes going by.

I told her abortion was an option but she wanted to keep

the baby. Her father had said as much on the phone too. 'The fruit of your karma isn't always sweet,' he had said cryptically after asserting that he wanted her to keep the child. I had expected him to disown her.

We talked for long over cups of tea and she told me all she remembered in a manner so frank it unnerved me. Sharmila wanted to talk, god knows for how long, and she must've found a sympathetic ear in Kumar. Listening to her talk with her fingers wrapped around the cup of tea, for one mad minute, I wondered if I could keep Sharmila with me. Maybe even marry her. But I dismissed it as easily as I considered it. They'd cast me out. If I lived elsewhere then maybe that wouldn't have mattered so much but here, in Kathmandu, where social ties run thicker and more matted than congealed blood, I wouldn't last. She wouldn't either.

I saw Sharmila and her father off at the Kalanki bus stop. She wore the red kurta and before she boarded the bus, she repeated, 'He loves me.'

This is where the story should end, as it does for so many others who come to Kathmandu. Bhupi Sherchan called this valley a cold ashtray, where people like Sharmila are stubbed out as easily as so many cigarettes. For anyone else, the story might have ended with a young girl waving goodbye from the bus window. But for Sharmila's sake, this one doesn't.

A few weeks later, at about ten at night, I got a frantic call from Raja.

'Kumar's gone,' he said. 'He left for school and never came back.'

I could hear the panic in his voice. 'Did you call the police?'

'Yes, but I don't know what they're doing.'

'Did he take anything?'

'He withdrew twenty thousand from my ATM and took all his clothes.' Raja's voice was breaking. 'He ran away.'

I went over to their house immediately. Rani was weeping uncontrollably amid various friends and relatives. Raja was constantly on the phone. I tried to comfort them the best I could but what exactly can you tell a man whose only son has just run away from home?

They never did find him either. The police reported after a few days that they suspected he had boarded a bus at Kalanki to the border but that was it. Raja and Rani called everyone they had any remote connection to for help, from politicians to army men. Kumar was just gone.

I don't think the Thapas ever considered that their son might have had someone to meet. I tried calling Krishna at the number Sharmila had used. There was no answer.

After a month, Raja, or shall I call him Ajay now, came back to work. He was visibly thinner and haggard. Even his glasses couldn't hide the bags under his eyes. I didn't bring up Kumar, or Rani, but it looked like they had patched things up. She brought him lunch sometimes and I would see them sitting in her car, just eating, not talking. Rani didn't seem the same either. Although she smiled at me a lot, the smiles never quite seemed to crinkle her eyes.

I considered telling them what I suspected but I never did. If I were to be cruel, they had brought this on themselves. Like one wise man had said, the fruit of your karma is not always sweet. I'd like to think Kumar met up with Sharmila, somewhere south of the border. I recall the flash of her eyes when she'd said, 'He loves me.' Maybe he did love her, in his own awkward adolescent manner. Maybe she loved him too, unabashedly. When they'd meet, he would be apologetic and she would be radiant.

I know it's a fairytale, but it doesn't hurt to dream.

The Presence of God

'You are such a perfect fool.' She said this to me in the middle of our argument. The argument that had begun early last night, the one that had continued through the night and into the morning, the one that we'd deferred for breakfast and while we met Hari and Trishna at Chakrapath Chowk, the one that had stayed deferred while we rode the microbus up to Budhanilkantha (although she made a point to sit on the seat farthest from me, which I'm sure Hari and Trishna noticed), the one that had restarted when we'd entered the Shivapuri National Park, walked for a good half-hour and begun to lag behind the others, the one that had begun when she'd asked, with no provocation at all, if I believed in god.

A fool, and a perfect one at that. The editor in her always knew to use apt, incisive words to slice like a knife through the heart.

I didn't really know how to respond. I tried to tell her that it wasn't that I didn't believe in god. It was just that I didn't care very much. To her that was worse. 'At least atheists believe in something,' she said. I then tried to concoct a whole spurious argument about how man can be moral without relying on a higher power to reward his morality.

Her riposte was instant and devastating. 'If you don't believe in something larger than yourself, you cannot be a moral person. Morality implies that there is a greater good and that circumstances are not isolated. You do something good because you believe it will have an effect greater than that of the immediate action. You have to believe that current events have a past and a future that exist outside of you and that you can implicitly trust. If not, you're just a narcissist.'

We argued on and off all night. We stopped three times to make tea. Twice, I boiled the tea while she readied the cups and once I did both while she pouted in the bedroom. I really didn't have an argument of my own. I just responded to her academically, but dishonestly. I didn't really believe in what I was saying. This was not something I had ever given much thought to. Growing up, I'd done what was expected of me, not because I'd believed in the expectations but because they were asked of me. And they were nothing large and existential. So I once fainted while standing in line at the Bhadrakali temple for three hours in the morning with no food or water. I considered that a small sacrifice, like the ones that everyone needed to make in a family. I'm certain that mother, the one who invariably led me to these temples once or twice every few months, didn't like making breakfast, lunch and dinner for my father and me every day, but she rarely complained. Like I said, small sacrifices.

It was not that my family was very religious. Mother and grandmother did their puja every morning and mother didn't enter the kitchen or the puja kotha during her time of the month. Temple visits were occasional and the family pandit visited on every proper occasion, usually on the death anniversary of grandfather. Father would then don a milky white lungi and go bare-chested except for a diagonal janai around his torso. That was the only time father would do anything religious, though. He never came to the temples with us and for every other household puja he had a ready excuse, which invariably was that he had 'work at the office'. Mother never pushed, she seemed content that I was willing to brave hordes of militant middle-aged women wielding sharp-edged steel trays laden with vermilion, rice, blackened sunflower seeds, an assortment of flowers and that bright yellow lather the name of which I always forget.

Eventually, and against all odds, I got older. And I wasn't ready anymore to hold mother's hand while crossing the road to the Mahankal temple. Large groups of women started to make me nervous and I began to protest outings, not just those to the temple but anywhere public that sparked acknowledgement in onlookers that I was walking down the street with my mother. Mother refused to relent at first but I had reached an age when I was perfectly happy to sulk alone in my room and not interact with her for days on end. Her periodic spells of the silent treatment, thus, failed to evoke the desired contrition in me. My sacrifices loomed much larger than hers anyway, or so I thought.

So the temple tours stopped and except for Guru Purnima, when I'd have to tie a supposedly 'holy' orange-yellow thread around my wrist, Dashain, where I'd have gobs of messy, runny tika on my forehead with itchy, inside-the-back-of-your-shirt jamara on my skull, and Tihar, where an assortment of short pujas often ended with firecrackers (this was before the Maoists started setting off real bombs), I managed to extricate myself from most other household religious practices.

Meera, on the other hand, was devout. And knowing that, I should have expected this argument (remember?) to have come up sooner or later. We'd been together then for maybe a year and a half, I can't recall clearly. But we never really were anniversary people—that was one of the things I'd liked about her. I do remember, though, that on our second date, we'd passed the Pashupati temple while on our way to Baneshwor on my bike and she'd instinctively put her hands together and bowed her head. This I spied in the bike's left rear-view mirror, which, though at a horrendously crooked angle, provided me with my first glimpse of religious Meera.

There were other things too. She fasted every Tuesday, and once, I'd accompanied her to the Tangal Ganesh temple at 5 a.m. in the morning to light 108 butter lamps because she'd prayed and asked for that editing job with the *Himal Times*. She'd received an email the previous night confirming her hiring and felt that it was only decent to thank the lord Ganesh for his benevolence. Hence the 108 butter lamps. I'd asked her why so many but she'd responded with some mumbo-jumbo about it being a holy number and all that. Frankly, it all sounded Sanskrit to me. And truthfully, I'd found the whole thing slightly bizarre, especially when I was lighting number fifty-three of the 108 butter lamps.

Meera had also built a prayer nook in our bedroom, with three small renderings—one Shiva and Parvati seated on a deerskin, palms out magnanimously; one Krishna with his flute to his mouth and his legs crossed daintily; and one Kali with her tongue out, trampling Shiva under her feet. Every morning, Meera would sit cross-legged in front of these frames with lit incense in between her folded palms and chant some unintelligible Sanskrit that she'd memorized (but could not tell me what it meant). Like mother, Meera did not go near the puja nook when she was on her period. But as a small concession to the modern age, she did cook when it was her turn (we alternated, before you start to tsk-tsk).

But she never asked me to do much either, and she never asked me about my beliefs. I brought this up during our argument.

'I always assumed you were religious in your own way,' was her reply. 'After all, you are a Bahun.'

So what had made her conclude that I was a truly godless man now?

'Because,' she said, 'your father just died and you didn't even shave your head.'

Two months ago, when I told my friends and co-workers that father had died, they'd all apparently assumed that I would shave my head, leaving an unseemly tuft of hair for a tuppee, and wear all white everything for a year (or was it thirteen days?). I didn't think father would have wanted me to shave my head and wear all white. He was very particular about his appearance, and by extension, mine, since how I looked reflected on him. So I had my first daura-suruwal tailored at the age of three and a fitted suit at the age of four; I learned how to tie a tie at five and I learned to match my shoes to my coat at six.

So I didn't shave my head nor did I wear white and, apparently, that had deeply offended Meera. She hadn't said anything before this but clearly it had been brewing inside of her. And Meera wasn't a fighting girl. She was very good at letting little things that did not matter slide. Like when I would forget to wash the dishes overnight, or when I'd forget to call her to tell her that I'd be going drinking with friends, or when I'd borrow her umbrella, forget to give it back and she'd end up getting wet in the rain. She was never hung up on differences and whenever I got mad at her, she was always conciliatory. She was really the first person on whom my irascibility did not seem to grate.

That's why this argument really surprised me. It caught me unawares, like that time at the Irish Pub in Lazimpat when I had gotten belligerently drunk and an equally belligerent young man had kicked me in the groin while I'd had my hands up expecting a punch. You could say that in over eighteen months of togetherness, we'd never really had a fight that continued past an hour or two. And that, too, mostly due to my stubbornness. But this, she was unwilling to let this go. And for the first time in over eighteen months of togetherness, I was a little afraid for us.

I knew that there was no way for me to satisfy her. She wasn't looking for an answer from me. I could tell she was trying to understand (that had always been her nature) but my way of being must have seemed completely contradictory to the way she understood the world. Meera had grown up in Dang with her mother and younger sister. Her father had passed away when she was seven and her mother, perhaps slightly more religious than my own, raised her under the shadow of a daal ladle. Meera would be locked in the bathroom until she'd learned her multiplication tables. Meera would receive swats from a stitch of sal wood whenever she misspelled English words. Meera would pray to the gods every night before going to bed, regardless of how the day had been.

So when she received a scholarship to study at Buddhanilkantha School in Kathmandu in Class 4, along with her army-green bedroll and her metal trunk of clothes, Meera carried over her mother's teachings.

The night of the argument we fell asleep at four in the morning. She slept facing away from me the entire time. When the argument restarted the next day, in between that Shivapuri quiet and calm, we were both very tired.

'Look,' went the opening salvo. 'You don't have to believe in god. Just tell me you believe in something bigger than yourself.'

'But that doesn't matter to me,' my return volley was already pathetic, I was pleading. 'It's not that I don't believe in something bigger. I just feel that it has very little bearing on who I am and what I do.'

'How can you not think about something like this?' she asked, seemingly flabbergasted. That was exactly how she'd asked me the same question last night. We were already starting to repeat ourselves.

Our argument devolved into shameless slander after that. It turned easily into a 'you said, I never said'. I expected that of myself but it was quite surprising to see her stoop to my level. But we had to stop, Hari and Trishna were waiting for us up ahead. He was leaning against the rocky hill that lined one side of the road we were walking on. She was towards the other grassy side where the sharp slope was peopled with thick underbrush and a few scattered trees. They had both come well-equipped for the hike, with expensive walking shoes, shorts, hats and sunglasses. Hari had even whipped out a fancy DSLR from his backpack and had it pointed at us.

We flashed fake smiles as best we could. They didn't seem to notice. Hari started up a conversation with Meera and Trishna started to walk with me. We made small talk, I wasn't very good friends with Trishna or Hari. They both worked with Meera at the newspaper. Hari was a copy editor and Trishna edited the features. They were both in their late twenties, and despite working at the same place in such close quarters, they had been together for close to five years.

They were a very good-looking couple, that much I must admit. Hari was from Biratnagar, dark, large-eyed, and with thick, sleek black hair that he kept parted severely to the right. Trishna was a Kathmandu Newar, brown, high-cheekboned, with a wide expressive face. Trishna liked to talk, but she wasn't annoying because she always had interesting things to say. Like when she stopped me to point out how this specific type of banmara creeper had all but killed a tree whose branches were hanging low under the weight of the parasite. I didn't know if she was right but she spoke with such authority that if she'd said the Buddha was born in India, she could've convinced me.

When we resumed walking, she started telling me about one specific contributor to the newspaper. This man would write frequently on a variety of topics. His ideas were mildly interesting but his English was passable. He seemingly wrote without an intuition for grammar—that instinct you build up after years of reading and writing that tells you to write this way and not that. Trishna would diligently fix all his subject-verb agreements, his dangling clauses, his run-on sentences, and his gerunds. (She would not fix any split infinitives because she didn't believe in them.) This man would quietly accept her fixes but if she ever slipped up, like a typo so glaring that even he could pick up, he would write her a condescending and patronizing email pointing out her mistake. Trishna was ranting. Her eyebrows were all the way up and her hands were gesturing wildly. It was quite an amusing sight.

Up ahead, Hari and Meera had stopped by a narrow path diverging off the road and into the upper slopes of the hill. 'There's a waterfall in here,' said Hari when we came within earshot. 'Do you want to go in?'

Trishna and I both nodded and the four of us made our way down the jungle path. It was a narrow one-person lane that led in between two large boulders jutting out from the slope. Trees leaned in at dangerous angles and sticky creepers hung down like dangling spiderwebs. As we walked, the machine-gun patter of water hitting rock grew louder and we came to the cascade. It was less impressive than we'd imagined. The water was little more than a gush and it barely fell ten metres. Nevertheless, we took off our shoes and dipped our feet in the small pool collecting at the bottom of the waterfall. Meera and I folded our pants legs while Hari and Trishna waded in, the water barely up to their knees.

As Hari and Trishna began to drift away, splashing water at each other, Meera and I sat close, not touching. I could feel her gaze on me but I continued to stare at the top of the waterfall, where I could make out a hardy green plant, a large weed maybe, on the left bank of the waterfall, constantly buffeted by the flow of water. It was only a matter of time before the plant would be ripped from its roots and deposited at the bottom of the very pool we had our feet in.

This was when she told me that I was a perfect fool (now we've come full circle). She said it easily, and again, I really didn't know how to respond. I was a fool because I didn't believe in the things that she believed in. The Meera I fell in love with would not have said that. But what did I know? Except for the fact that people are always changing and you have to learn to love new things about them in new ways. If (or more often, when) you find yourself unable to do this, then it's time to part ways.

'And you know why?' she continued, even though I didn't really want to know why. 'Because you're naïve. You've never been in a situation where you've needed god, that's why you think you can do without him.'

'Like when you needed your job at the *Himal Times*?' I felt mean-spirited.

She shot me a poisonous look. 'When my mother was dying, I prayed ten times a day. Not to save her, but to take her. She had cancer and it was all over the place. There was no saving her but she could've been saved all that pain. You've never been in a situation like that.'

She had a point. I really hadn't been in a situation so

desperate. Even as a kid, I very rarely prayed for anything. I remember once, in Class 4, lying on the top bunk of my hostel bed, I'd prayed that the last white pair of socks that I thought I had lost would be miraculously found.

And lo, I found them balled up in a corner of my clothes shelf the next day. But then I was so happy to not have to wear blue school socks to play football that I forgot all about thanking god.

I mumbled something unintelligible to Meera in response. Thankfully, Hari and Trishna came back towards us.

'Have you guys been fighting?' Trishna asked, always the intuitive one. Actually, she'd probably seen the thundercloud gathered on Meera's brows.

'No, it's just a stupid argument,' Meera said sweetly, her face, posture and tone of voice all changing effortlessly.

'Well, we'd like to go up the side of the waterfall,' Trishna said. 'Hari says there's a bigger pond and a bigger waterfall some ways up.'

So we followed Hari single file, not really talking. The walk, or rather the climb, was strenuous. More than following a path, Hari was making one. He scrambled over logs and bushes and pulled himself up by weeds and shrubs. We tried to mimic his actions the best we could but it was a tough crawl. After maybe half an hour of clawing at flimsy roots and shoots, Meera finally snapped.

'Hari, where exactly is this waterfall?'

Hari yelled something back about it being just up ahead after a small plateau but I didn't quite catch what he said. I was too busy scrambling for a handhold after the weed I'd just relied on to support my weight had callously betrayed me.

Another few dozen minutes passed in the same fashion. Meera, who was in front of me, was really struggling, her breath coming in sharp gasps, like an obese person climbing up a flight of stairs. The jungle had grown thicker around us and the slope seemed to have gotten steeper. There was no sign of a plateau.

Hari halted at a large tree with a Y-fork. He looked to the left and to the right. Then he looked back down past me and the way we had just come. I did not take this as a sign of confidence.

Fortunately, I wasn't the only one who'd noticed Hari's confusion. Trishna and Meera both began to assault Hari with admonishments, all some variation of 'we are lost' and 'you are an idiot'.

I wanted to help Hari, as a fellow male, but the guy had no defence. Meera was already angry with me and I couldn't risk Trishna's wrath too. 'It should have been here,' was among the worst things Hari could've said but he said it anyway, and repeatedly.

After Trishna and Meera had exhausted themselves vocally, we decided, collectively, to head back down the way we came, following the messy path we'd just created. This time Trishna would lead the way (she decided this herself).

Downhill was not much easier than uphill. I slipped and slid, locking my knees so that I wouldn't end up somersaulting over Hari, Meera and Trishna, as somehow I'd ended up last once again. There was no talking except for our grunts, wheezes and gasps. We went on like this for quite some time. When I finally found an even surface to rest and look at my watch, it had been over an hour that we'd been descending.

We stopped at a clearing of sorts, a semi-circular space in between eight giant chir trees. The air was sweet with resin and the ground underneath crunched with pine needles. Trishna had stopped, exhausted, and Meera was sitting with her back against a tree trunk. Hari was just standing around, looking sheepish. I checked my phone and, as expected, found no signal.

We had walked for more than two hours into the forest. There was no doubt about the fact that we were hopelessly lost. I didn't even know Shivapuri had forests that went on forever like this. From the outside, all it seemed like was a hill, and not a very big one at that.

I sat down beside Meera. 'Is this the kind of desperate situation you were talking about earlier?' I couldn't resist.

'Please don't,' she said tiredly.

I relented. I could tell she was worried.

'What do we do now?' said Trishna eventually.

No one really had an answer. We ate a Snickers bar each and drank up most of the water we had brought with us. Clearly, none of us had ever been in a situation like this before, or we'd have known to save our water.

'Does anyone have a signal on their phone?' Trishna asked.

We all checked. Not a single bar on anyone's phone.

'You guys stay here, I'll look around,' I volunteered, figuring I might as well do something.

'No.' Meera was not having it. 'You are not wandering off so we can get separated and even more lost. Let's try to figure out where to go first.'

Meera had only just spoken when we all heard a sound,

like those you hear in horror films before someone gets horribly mauled. We all raised our heads, waiting like deer caught in headlights.

Something was thrashing through the underbrush off to the right of where Hari had been leaning against a tree. Leaves were rustling, twigs were crunching and a body was coming closer. Instinctively, like the herd animals we were, we huddled. It was definitely an animal and we were all hoping, maybe some of us even praying, that it wasn't a leopard.

The noise stopped. 'Who's there?' a man called out in clear Nepali. '*Ae, ko cha tya?*'

Trishna was the first to gather her wits together. '*Dai? Ae, dai?*' I was still dry-mouthed.

The brush parted and a man appeared, short and squat, old, and clad in a daura-suruwal with a Gurung bhangra around him. 'Where did you come from?' He seemed as surprised to see us as we were to see him.

'We got lost,' Trishna said, always ready to take charge. 'We've been walking for two hours. Can you show us the way back to the road?'

'The road?' The man repeated. 'Pitch road? Not around here. You have to go back.'

'We don't know how to get back. Can you take us?' I asked, finally finding my voice, buttressed by Trishna.

The man seemed to get even more perplexed, scratching his hair, which, despite his wrinkled old-man face, was thick and jet black. And despite the bhangra, he didn't look Gurung at all, I noticed. He had wide, large eyes with deep crow's feet around the edges and a pronounced hook nose.

'Okay, follow me closely,' he said, seemingly coming to a conclusion and immediately turning back into the forest. We hurried behind him, with me, once again, at the very tail end.

Following this man was even worse than following Hari. Now there was thick underbrush involved and branches that those in front kept swinging into my face. The man walked fast and purposefully and it was getting difficult keeping up. He didn't once look behind him.

We walked steadily through the forest, leapt over a small rivulet bubbling among the roots of trees, and clambered across a few rocky outcroppings. No one said anything, we were concentrating on not losing this man. But I couldn't help but wonder where exactly this man was leading us. The areas we were walking through didn't look at all familiar and this man, too, like that fool Hari earlier, seemed to be simply making his own way.

I had started to really tire when we finally came out of the forest. But there was no sign of a road. The treeline ended onto a wide dirt clearing and up ahead were three or four houses. Behind them, and disturbingly close, the forest began again. The houses were two-storey, mostly mud, rock and wood. Each house, identical, had a small porch with a thatched overhang and two windows peering out. It was as quaint a Nepali hamlet as the ones that appeared as illustrations in Class 8 social studies textbooks. As far as I could see, there was no path leading into this little hamlet and no path leading out.

I started to feel strangely claustrophobic, in a way I hadn't felt in the forest. There we were in the midst of trees. Here we were hemmed in by trees, like a vast, forbidding fence that rose metres high. When Meera placed her hand in mine, I knew I wasn't the only one who was uncomfortable.

The old man had started walking towards the houses as we stood gawking. 'What's on the other side of Shivapuri?' asked Hari. 'I think we might have climbed over. What village is this?'

None of us had an answer so we simply followed the old man. He stopped at the first house and sat down on the porch. The houses were eerily silent. There was no one around—not a single child playing, not a single woman tending cooking fires and not a single man lounging lazily in the sun. There was no sound of chicken, goats or cows either. I couldn't spy a single wire, electric or telephone.

'Dai, kun gaun ho yo?' Trishna finally asked.

'It's my home,' the man replied cryptically.

'Are we still in Kathmandu? What district is this?' Hari now.

'Kathmandu is far away.' The old man had taken off his bhangra and was reaching into it, searching around for something.

'Can we get a bus to Kathmandu from here then?'

'No, no bus.' He brought out a pack of beedis, tied with a crimson string. He fished out a worn pack of Tir matches and lit his smoke.

'Then why did you bring us here? We need to get back to Kathmandu.' Trishna was starting to get frustrated but I could tell she was trying to keep it under control. This man was our only hope of finding our way and it wouldn't do to piss him off.

'Sit here a while. Smoke, drink water, rest.' The man blew large clouds of sweet-smelling smoke into the quiet, tranquil air.

Trishna made an exasperated sound and sat down a ways from the man. Hari took out his camera and began to wander round the place. Meera and I followed, our hands still clasped. A single dark opening led inside each home, none with a door. They were like gaping mouths, waiting for the unwary to enter. I tried to peer inside but the depths were dark as charcoal. There were only four houses in total, each opening to a central open space. They were all close together too; you could've leapt from one thatched roof to the next.

'Where is everyone?' Hari asked out loud to no one in particular. 'This is kind of scary,' he said, giving voice to my thoughts.

Meera and I wandered off on our own, leaving Hari to scout out haunted house scenes to take pictures of. We walked towards the house furthest from us, calling out before peering into the dark entrance.

'Dai? Didi? *Koi cha?*' I yelled.

There was no answer so we stepped over the entrance block and inside the house. The inside was just as eerie, silent and warm with the saccharine smell of wet straw. There was a mud chulo in the corner, three logs sticking out like in a picture perfect postcard of rural life. In the opposite corner was a wooden staircase leading to the second floor. Meera disengaged herself from me and took the stairs up while I continued to look around. There were a number of rolled up straw sukuls in the corner and a low wooden bed with a thin mattress. I sat down on the bed and a cloud of dust rose up around me. The bed looked like it hadn't been used in a long time. There also weren't any signs of daily life, no milk or leftover food and a gagri in the corner which had no water. I walked over to the only window and threw it open, finally letting more light in.

'Can you come here?' Meera called from above, her voice echoing through the stillness.

Upstairs it was brighter, light streaming in through two wide windows. On straw mats laid out neatly on the floor lay Meera, spread-eagled.

'I'm so tired,' she said.

'What is this place?' I asked.

'Khoi,' she replied, rolling over on her left side. 'I'm going to take a nap.'

'Have you lost your mind?'

'Come on. Just five minutes. And then we can go talk to that budo again.'

She had closed her eyes and was already starting to breathe deeply when I lay down beside her. I wasn't planning on sleeping, just rest a while and then wake Meera up in five minutes, although I knew she would be cranky. I closed my eyes and found myself drifting off to sleep in a stranger's house.

I woke up, being shaken roughly. I jerked upright, uncomprehending. It was Hari, whispering my name urgently.

'What happened?' I asked. 'How long have I been asleep?'

The light was gone. In the twilight haze, I made out Trishna and Meera off to the side and Hari's face in front of me, wide-eyed and staring.

'Something's happening,' he said.

'How is it evening already? How long did I sleep?' I asked again.

'We fell asleep too,' Hari replied. 'I took some pictures and went back to Trishna. She said the old man had gone to the back of the house to take a leak. She was sitting leaning against the wall with her eyes closed. I did the same, just to rest for a while, and when I woke up, evening.'

It was then that I heard the commotion. Hari was whispering and, in the backdrop, there was a muted chorus of voices, feet pattering and a mess of movement.

'What's happening outside?' I asked.

'We don't know. There's a whole bunch of people, maybe almost a hundred. I have no idea where they came from. When Trishna and I woke up, there were a bunch of people just looking at us. We tried to talk to them but none of them replied. That old man was gone so we looked for you two,' said Hari.

I stood and went to the window. Outside, in the open clearing, there were a great many people, all dressed differently, in clothes that seemed oddly stereotypical of their cultures. There were no women or children, only men. Some of them were leading goats, cows and buffaloes while others had chicken or some fruit cradled in their hands. They were all gathered around a three-foot-high wooden pole that clearly hadn't been there when we got there. Red and white ribbons, like the twins you use during pujas, fluttered in a non-existent breeze. One man, topless and in a white lungi, was liberally smearing vermilion on the pole.

'They're doing a puja,' I said.

'Looks like it,' said Meera from next to me. She was crowding me at the window while Hari and Trishna were at the other.

'Do you think I can take pictures?' asked Hari, whipping out his camera.

'No flash!' Meera hissed at him.

The priest finished anointing the pole and sat off to one side, legs crossed. The traditional accoutrements of a puja were absent. There was no all-consuming fire and no mumbled chanting. The priest simply sat there, his lips unmoving. The crowd was murmuring within itself but it sounded more like conversation than anything religious. The only sharp sound piecing the lull was Hari's camera shutter as he snapped picture after picture from the window.

All of these people had to come from somewhere, I reasoned with myself, remembering that we were lost and our guide had disappeared. After the puja, we can just ask them for directions to a bus, I figured.

It started to get dark rapidly and I found myself straining to see clearly. The priest finally lit a small fire next to the pole and gestured towards the crowd. The men parted neatly and a large man carrying an equally large, evil khukuri appeared, leading a massive he-goat. The thing was huge, almost up to the man's chest, with a long, scraggly beard and thick, curly horns. I could almost smell him from the window—that acrid, unwashed stench.

Another man came forward and took hold of the rope around the he-goat's neck. From behind, another man held its back legs. The priest rose with a small lota of water and splashed some directly onto the goat's face. The goat didn't move, only bleated mournfully as if it was aware of the fate awaiting it. The priest sprinkled more water and the goat shivered, a tremor running through its body. The priest gave way and the large man raised his khukuri high, paused, and brought it down mightily on the goat's neck, severing it neatly with a solid thwack. The priest quickly grabbed the head by the horns and anointed the pole with the fresh gushing blood.

Now the rest of the people started to come up, tying the ropes of their goats, cows and buffaloes to the pole and leaving them there. The chicken too were deposited at the base of the pole. Everyone huddled around and the low murmur dissipated. Everyone went silent, except for the clucking of the chicken and an occasionally bleating goat. The silence went on for about ten minutes, all of us afraid to break it with even a whisper.

Then, from the far end, movement. The crowd was slowly parting again, making way for someone approaching from the back. The people at the very front stepped aside and from the mass of men emerged a band of animals. At least they seemed to be animals. The light was almost gone so I couldn't see very clearly but I made out a shamble of several large animals, the size of fully grown German Shepherd dogs, but with a lot more fur, like that of a Lhasa Apso. A snout, narrower and longer than that of a dog, emerged from underneath the fur with a longer tongue, thick and reddish, snaking out constantly. Instead of paws, their feet were double-jointed, with the front end resting flat on the ground like that of the Egyptian sphinx.

Their gait was awkward, a slow shuffling crawl forward. They looked like hideously deformed Chimeras. From next to me, I heard Meera's sharp intake of breath and her hand found mine again.

The animals gathered around the pole, their tongues lapping at the blood from the sacrificed goat. Then they started to eat, the snouts coming apart into two sharp fanged jaws. The dead goat was eaten in a matter of minutes, bones ground inside massively powerful jaws. The rest of the livestock shrank in fear, attempting to get away from the advancing animals. But the men barred their way, throwing the chicken back as they tried to escape. The crowd was close and frenzied now and it was getting even more difficult for me to see, but the sounds made what was happening evident. There were mournful bleats and sharp squawks as goats, cows, buffaloes and chicken were torn into. There were grunts and snorts, the likes of which I had never heard before. Jaws snapped and bones cracked.

It was over quickly. The hundred or so livestock offerings were gone, as if inhaled rather than chewed and swallowed. The creatures looked around, sniffing the air with their snouts. Finding little else to eat, they shuffled back through the crowd, which itself began to disperse. Around the pole, remnants of skin, bone and blood littered the ground. As we watched, the men disappeared into the forest and out of our sight. No one entered the house we were in.

It was then that I realized Meera's nails were digging into the back of my hand. I jerked my hand away painfully, coming to my senses. The movement seemed to break Meera's stupor also.

'What the hell?' she whispered in English.

'Wait,' I remembered and forced myself away from the window. Using my phone for illumination, I rushed down the stairs and out the door. It was too late. Somehow, in less than a minute, more than a hundred people had disappeared.

'Dai? Dai?' I called out, but there was no reply. I walked towards the pole, hoping that at least the priest was around. Only the fire still burned. The smell of murder was thick in the air, along with warm, sickly blood mixed with the rank odour of eviscerated flesh. I carefully avoided the pools of blood while looking around. There were deep paw prints in the ground where the animals had stood. Impossible four-fingered claw marks sunk deep into the dry, packed earth.

I walked back to the house and climbed the stairs. No one had followed me out. Trishna and Hari were huddled on the floor, arms around each other and Meera was at the window, looking vacantly out. I put my arm around her shoulder and she jumped at my touch.

No one wanted to talk right then and I didn't even make the attempt. Sometime later, I don't know when, we fell asleep again.

When I awoke, morning light was streaming through the windows. Meera was asleep with her arm around my waist but Hari and Trishna were nowhere to be seen. I woke Meera and we made our way outside. In the clearing, the pole was still there but the flesh and bones had been carried away in the night, probably by scavenging birds and foxes. We found Hari and Trishna back at the first house, sitting next to the old man from earlier.

'You just left us yesterday,' I said to the old man as I walked up. I was angry.

'Hey, I was just about to come wake you up,' said Trishna. 'This guy says he left because Hari and I fell asleep and wouldn't wake up no matter how much he tried. He couldn't find you guys so he went his own way. I already yelled at him but you can yell at him some more,' she offered.

'Can he get us out of here?' I didn't want to argue or fight. It had been a strange night and I only wanted to get back to familiarity.

'He says the road is just an hour's walk from here,' Trishna said.

'Did you ask him about last night?' The smell and sounds were just coming back to me.

'He says he has no idea what puja that was,' Hari replied.

I asked the old man myself, describing the creatures. He appeared puzzled at first but then cracked into a smile, thinking we were playing a joke on him. He honestly appeared to have no idea. I showed him the blood stains on the pole and on the ground, but he brushed them off as remnants from an earlier puja. I asked him where everyone who lived in these houses was. He simply replied that they were working in the fields. The man was a cipher, and I soon realized no further information would be forthcoming. Exasperated, I gave up.

Soon, once again, we were following the budo through the forest.

But, after an hour's walk, true to his word, we came to a road and I recognized where we were. We hadn't even left the Shivapuri National Park. The monastery inside the park was a half-hour walk uphill and we could easily be out of here in a few hours of brisk walking. I turned to thank the old man but he was already heading back into the forest.

We followed the road back down, talking along the way. I don't think any of us was ready to articulate just what had happened, but Hari had taken pictures so we crowded around his DSLR to take a look. He hadn't used flash, afraid to attract attention, so the pictures were grainy and dark. We could make out the people and the priest, even the livestock and the poultry tied to the pole. But no creatures. It was too dark around where they had gathered and except for what looked like a snout or a paw, there was nothing to go on.

Trishna described the animals as having thick leathery skin, like water buffaloes. She described large eyes and a long snout, just like I had seen. Hari too claimed to have seen no fur but no snout either. Just jaws and teeth, wide and large, made for ripping apart meat. Meera refused to say anything. I kept asking her but all she would say was she didn't know what she saw.

We parted ways at Maharajgunj Chowk. We were all hungry, tired and imbued with a vague sense of foreboding. Meera and I didn't talk all the way back to our apartment. Our argument about god had been forgotten in the light of the inexplicable. She stepped directly into the bathroom and was in there for close to an hour. When she came out, she had showered and washed but her eyes were red and puffy, as if she'd been staying up all night, or crying. I asked her if anything was wrong but she only said that she didn't want to talk and went into our room. I heard her put some music on and start to tap away at her computer keyboard.

166 *City of Dreams*

We ate leftover food and stayed in all day, me watching TV shows and she on her computer. What exactly had we seen? Those weren't any creatures I'd even seen before. They were a haphazard hodgepodge of something you'd expect to see in a poorly thought-out fantasy novel or in some twisted child's imagination. Or maybe it had been the darkness playing tricks on us. Maybe those people were worshipping leopards or dogs of some kind. Maybe they'd just sacrificed those animals en masse, like they do during Dashain every year or during the Gadhimai festival every five years. Snouts and teeth could have been khukuris and khudas.

But they weren't. I know all four of us saw something, so it wasn't a hallucination or a figment of my imagination. And it certainly wasn't just the lack of light. I remember the animals. I even remember their sounds, the wheezing as they shuffled forward, and their smell, sharp and foul, like ruined eggs. When I saw those creatures, and I'm certain I saw them, I must confess here that I did pray. For a second, however fleeting, I turned to god. Because I was afraid and it wasn't a fear I had even known before. It wasn't the fear of an evil man out to do me wrong. It wasn't the fear of death or abandonment. It was a fear similar to what I had once felt when I was a child and I'd lost sight of my mother at Bishalbazaar. It was a fear that was total and all-consuming, when you don't know what or where anything is. It was like being turned around and around and then asked to get comfortable with the world as it spun around you. It was the fear of a world out of whack.

I also found myself suddenly much more amenable to Meera's side of the argument. After all, what is god but the indescribable, the inexplicable, the un-understandable. Maybe even the transcendental—something that we in this evanescent world are unable to comprehend.

Something seemed to change for Meera too. She refused to talk to me about that night and she never again brought up our argument. The next morning she did not come out with a lit stick of incense to offer the gods at her puja corner. She did not kneel in front and chant her verse. She did not offer water and flowers. Meera did not pray. Shiva-Parvati, Krishna and Kali all stared balefully at her whenever she passed but she barely glanced at them, as if purposefully avoiding their accusatory gaze.

I didn't push the matter. Instead, on rare mornings, I found myself placing a flower before Shiva-Parvati and, on occasion, even found myself touching my forehead whenever I passed by Pashupati. I might have been a perfect fool but I figured, the sooner you make peace with the inexplicable, the better.

The Child

'It's a dog,' Seema said to herself. '*Kukkur, kukkur, kukkur*. It's just a dog.'

There had been a thud, followed by two bumps. The thud was muted and firm, a soft yielding body striking hard, impassable metal. Then two rough bumps that jolted her around in her seat as her car climbed up and over the body. She'd seen something from the corner of her eye, a flash of warm colour rushing against the cold grey of concrete. Her body had reacted instinctively, her foot plunging down onto the brake pedal, her hands turning the steering wheel away and outward. But the impact had been fast and final. In the rear-view mirror the body lay slumped and unmoving.

The evening sky was crimson and there was no one else on the street. Ahead, in the distance, Seema spied the blue outline of a peanut vendor's mobile stall, a curl of smoke rising lazily from it. Other than that, this stretch of road, pockmarked with potholes, was deserted. No elderly men idling on bamboo stools and sipping tea, no enthusiastic game of carom among youths and wife-beaters, no middle-aged women leaning against shop counters. And no other children.

Seema stared at the mirror, her triceps trembling even as

her hands clutched the steering wheel so tight her knuckles were turning white. She wanted to get out and look, but, instead, she found herself shifting the car from neutral. She was hearing white noise, a monotone that emanated in her head and escaped out her ears. She drove home mechanically, hands shifting gears and feet pumping pedals. She surveyed herself, as if from afar, while she drove. The nails on her hands bright, her hair coming loose from a ponytail, her mouth a tight, straight line.

She parked next to the gate to her house and just sat there for a while. She contemplated not going inside but she had nowhere else to be. Inside Dinesh was in the kitchen making dinner. She could smell frying cauliflower and potatoes but she felt no appetite. Dinesh didn't hear her come in. He was bent over the karai, stirring furiously. She slumped onto the living room's only couch, reaching reflexively for the remote.

'I didn't hear you come in,' Dinesh glanced over from the kitchen when he heard the television turn on. 'Was the gate open?'

Seema didn't respond. Her eyes were glued to the screen where a singing competition was currently playing out on the Sony channel.

'Was the gate open?' Dinesh asked again, louder this time.

When he still didn't receive an answer, he covered the karai with a steel plate and came over.

'*Ke bhayo?* Why aren't you talking?' He sat down next to her and almost recoiled when he saw her face. She looked haggard. The hand holding the remote was trembling.

'What happened?' Dinesh asked again, more urgently this time, taking her hand in his.

'I think I ran over a dog,' Seema replied shakily.

Dinesh made soothing sounds, draping his arms around his wife's shoulders. Seema leaned into him, burying her head in his chest. She thought she would cry, but no tears came. She felt hollow, as if her insides had been neatly scooped out.

'Did it die?' Dinesh asked.

'I don't know,' Seema replied, her words muffled against Dinesh's T-shirt, which reeked of besar. She raised her head and saw that the tips of his right hand were stained yellow.

'It's okay, Seema. It was probably just a stray dog,' Dinesh tried to console her. 'Wouldn't have lived very long anyway.'

Dinesh made her a cup of black tea when he went back to check on the vegetables. Seema stared vacantly at the television, not registering the drama unfolding on screen as a young contestant, barely a child, was unceremoniously eliminated from the competition. She felt nauseous and the tea didn't help much.

Dinner was a silent affair. Dinesh was usually a good cook, but this time he'd over-salted the daal. Seema tried her best to eat.

'There's too much salt in the daal,' Dinesh absently commented.

Seema only murmured her assent.

In bed, Dinesh cuddled close but Seema was in no mood. He gave up after a while, turned over and started to snore quietly. Seema lay awake for a long time in the darkness. In her two years of driving, it was the first time she'd hit anything. The Suzuki Alto she drove, which her father had bought her as a wedding gift, was still practically new, as she only used it to get to work and back. She didn't speed and was always mindful of potholes and speed breakers. Even as a young girl riding to college on her scooter, she had never gotten into a single accident. Quite a surprise, considering how traffic in Kathmandu was like navigating a daily stampede. Seema felt safer in her car, but she'd also take scrupulous care to avoid errant motorbikes and overtaking microbuses. As she closed her eyes, the wet sound of the impact seemed to reverberate in her ears. It was hours before she drifted off into a deep, dreamless sleep.

She couldn't drive the next day. She got into her car, which was still parked outside of her compound, and stared at the steering wheel. Her heart started to beat faster and her limbs began to tremble. She began to shake in her driver's seat and had to put her head on the steering wheel, close her eyes and take breath after deep breath before she finally calmed down. After about ten minutes of silent, nervous contemplation, she decided to take a bus to work.

It had been years since she'd taken a bus and it took her long to even figure out the route from home in Baluwatar to her office in Sanepa. The microbus she got onto was packed and claustrophobic. The conductor stood very close, smacking the side of the vehicle and yelling 'Lazimpat, Lainchaur, Jamal, Ghantaghar, Buspark' in a cadence. From her seat facing the wrong way on the microbus, she absently scanned the faces opposite her and delighted in the variety present. An abundance of ethnicities stared back at her, from the pale-faced, small-eyed, long-haired young man in the back with headphones to the square-jawed, wide-eyed man in a Dhaka topi to the dark, bushy-haired lady sitting in the front seat with a child on her lap. The kid, maybe five years old, met her eyes and stared unabashedly. Seema was overcome by a sense of nausea and stolidly avoided his gaze. When she got off at Ratnapark, she felt relief wash over her like a cooling breeze.

She boarded another, bigger microbus to Jawalakhel and got off outside the Pulchowk fire engine. She walked fast, heels clacking on newly laid concrete and her handbag swinging erratically as she weaved to avoid gaping holes and mounds of dirt from a construction project that never seemed to end.

Shyam the guard was cordial as ever, saying namaste and good morning. Seema replied the best she could, flashing a forced smile. At her desk things got better. The year was ending and the NGO she worked for had its yearly budget report due. It was Seema's job to consolidate all of the year's big bills and crunch all the numbers, making sure everything added up. It was tedious work, but something that required all of her attention.

Seema had always been good with numbers. She felt comfortable around them, with their indefatigable logic and their unbreakable rules. It wasn't like with Dinesh sometimes, who was an academic-turned-artist, currently unemployed. Dinesh had a Masters in Arts and Aesthetics from Jawaharlal Nehru University and liked to talk about the violence inherent in the colour crimson, the rational hegemony of the straight line and the oppressive nature of angular form. After three stints teaching art at colleges across Kathmandu, he had given up teaching to pursue his own art full time. Seema never quite understood what Dinesh was talking about but she liked his art, especially the one abstract painting he had made for her while they were still courting. In it her eyes occupy most of her face and her nose and lips are non-existent. Dinesh had always loved her large eyes with their dark, thick lashes, which always gave the impression that she was wearing eyeliner even when she wasn't. That painting now hung above their bed.

She'd been working for a couple of hours when Kaushal made his entrance. The door was flung open and Kaushal breezed in to a sea of hellos and how-are-yous. Like he did every day, he stopped to flirt with Rojina, the receptionist. He had a habit of sliding up onto Rojina's desk and talking down to her as she looked up at him from her chair. Rojina, a quiet Newar girl from Patan, would get visibly embarrassed at Kaushal's flirtations. She would blush, darkening her face further, and look away, breaking eye contact. When she smiled or laughed, she made certain to shield her teeth with her palm.

Kaushal was a consultant for the NGO and though he had no real work at the office, he was seemingly always there. The rumour making the rounds was that Kaushal was the chief's cousin and had been hired at an exorbitant salary for something nebulous. Kaushal was young and handsome, though short, and recently returned from the US. He'd lived in America for eight years and, as if to demonstrate, he felt the need to switch constantly between English and Nepali in conversation.

'Did you do something to your hair?' Kaushal's voice floated over to Seema, even as she tried harder to concentrate on the work before her. The expenses for last March did not seem to add up to all of the receipts that she had filed away and she was having difficulty tallying them. She was rifling through the bills when her breath caught in her throat and she felt like she was going to faint. Tucked in between the bills was a postcard from one of her partner NGOs, wishing her a happy Dashain. On the front was a picture of a child, maybe three or four years old, smiling widely at the camera from his mother's lap. Seema stared, a lump caught in her throat.

It was right then that Kaushal decided to come up from behind and violently shake her chair, jolting her out of her stupor. Seema screamed. When Rojina came running over to see what the matter was, Seema was sitting on the floor of her cubicle, her arms around her knees, shaking furiously. Kaushal was standing off to one side, frowning, and making small comforting noises.

'*Ke bhayo?*' Rojina asked, concerned.

'I didn't do anything,' Kaushal said immediately.

'Seema?' Rojina bent down and gingerly placed her hand on Seema's arm.

Seema flinched.

'What's wrong? Are you okay?'

Seema took a deep breath and looked up, 'Sorry, you just really scared me.'

'My god,' Kaushal broke into a smile. 'I thought I'd done something terrible.'

Seema stood shakily, balancing herself against the wall of the cubicle.

'Come, let's have tea,' Kaushal offered. 'You'll feel better.'

Rojina, convinced Kaushal had the situation under control, walked back to her desk.

At their regular tea shop, Kaushal took Seema's hands in his. 'What happened there? I thought I really hurt you.'

'*Kei hoina*, I just got scared,' Seema said, avoiding his gaze.

Kaushal's fingers were entwined with hers now and their warmth gave her comfort. Her heart was still pounding furiously and her legs felt unsteady, but Kaushal was there, gazing so attentively at her with his large, brown eyes that were so much like her own.

'Do you have a lot of work?' he asked.

Seema didn't answer. She knew the question that would follow in response to her answer and now, of all times, she didn't feel like answering.

The tea came in two small cups, hot and frothing. The lady who brought it over was squat and heavyset, her fingernails chipped and broken, her palms lined and rough. Seema looked at her own hands as Kaushal caressed them. Soft, smooth and unbroken, hands that had barely seen a day's work. Kaushal's were similar, except for the hard calluses on the tips of his fingers from playing guitar. Here they were, she thought to herself, two privileged people doing privileged things.

'I have a lot to do today, Kaushal,' she finally answered and took back her hands.

She didn't look up at Kaushal, though she could tell he was disappointed. He didn't say anything in reply, just picked up his tea and sipped it noisily.

Seema didn't want to admit it but Kaushal, like her numbers, comforted her. He was brash, arrogant and overbearing, but when he talked to you, he looked straight at you, straight into your eyes, as if he were looking for a way into your being. Seema felt naked in front of him, the way he searched her face as if looking for an answer. When they sat together like this, often with her hand in his, she felt as if everything else had fallen away.

She started from his fingers, his long, musician fingers that wrapped the teacup tightly, his forearms, muscled and thick, the shirtsleeves rolled up to his elbows, his shoulders, broad and even, his neck, smooth and open, his mouth, slightly parted lips, the irregular teeth, the slightly hooked nose and those piercing eyes.

When Kaushal first came to the office, Seema had found him cloying and irritating. He flirted openly with all the women and did not hesitate to reach out and touch arms and shoulders. And though Rojina seemed smitten with him from the very first day, Seema made it a point to keep him at a distance. This only seemed to encourage Kaushal. At first, he was overly complimentary, but confronted with Seema's ice, he changed tack—he started to tease her. Soft, stupid targets at first. He would crack jokes about her cubicle and how far away it was from everything else, as if someone intentionally wanted to keep her away from everyone else. He would comment on all the papers that lay strewn on her desk and would sarcastically ask if she needed help cleaning up. He would stand behind her as she drafted proposals and would pointedly call out her typos. When all of this only seemed to anger Seema, Kaushal changed tack again. Harder targets now. Her nail polish had been chipped for over a week; the tortoise clip that she used to tie back her hair was so old it had lost all its colour; the Louis Vuitton bag she carried was clearly fake; her old haircut looked much nicer than the new one; her last report contained upwards of six glaring errors besides sixteen typos.

This continued for quite some time. Seema did not give Kaushal much thought, despite wondering just why he was choosing to pick on her. It was a conversation with Rojina over lunch one day that changed the way she thought.

Rojina was distraught that day and Seema was trying to console her. Her boyfriend of three years had just broken up with her and Rojina had spent the last two days crying her eyes dry, leaving deep dark circles under her eyes. Rojina complained and cried and Seema did her best to listen and offer advice.

'Forget him, a pretty girl like you will find someone else in minutes,' Seema offered.

'Khoi? No one even looks at me,' Rojina complained.

'What about Kaushal?' Seema asked. 'He's always flirting with you. You should go for a date.'

'Kaushal?' Rojina snorted. 'He only has eyes for you.'

Seema nearly choked on the water she was sipping. 'Are you joking? He hates me.'

'Don't pretend, Seema. You know what's going on.'

'*Ke bhanira?* He's always so mean to me.'

'*Jiskira ho,* he's only joking.'

'That's joking? He constantly makes fun of the way I look, the clothes I wear, my work, everything.'

'Come on, Seema. He notices everything about you.'

Since then Seema couldn't help but look up every time Kaushal entered the office. She found herself laughing at his jokes and making fun of him right back. She commented on his mismatched socks, his scuffed shoes, his uneven hair and his penchant for always rolling up his sleeves, like some wannabe Bollywood hero.

It didn't take long for them to become friends. Smoothly and without even knowing it, they started to use 'ta' and 'tero' instead of 'timi' and 'timro'. What happened next was just as easy. The office had gone out to Thamel for a Dashain party right before the annual break. Pleasantly drunk, Kaushal and Seema shared a taxi home. It was late, past midnight, and in the dark of the cab, speeding through the city proper, they kissed. Seema was hesitant at first but eventually she relaxed. He pulled her close and she could feel the heat of his body. She put her hand on his neck and found herself forcing him closer. They only sprang apart embarrassed when the taxi driver pointedly asked which way to turn from Baluwatar Chowk.

Dinesh came to the door in his pyjamas when Seema rang the bell, her lipstick still smudged. Dinesh didn't comment or, perhaps, in the dim light of the moon, he didn't notice. By the time he had locked the doors and come back to bed, Seema had already undressed and gotten under the covers. She was drunk and amorous and Dinesh never noticed anything amiss.

The next day Seema and Kaushal both pretended like nothing had happened, but Kaushal, whenever it was just the two of them, took to holding her hand. Seema never protested. In the two months since that first kiss, nothing else happened between the two of them. Kaushal always asked her out for a drink but Seema never took him up on it. And though she had never even considered telling Dinesh what had happened, she felt guilty.

It wasn't that Dinesh and Seema had a bad relationship. Though their marriage had been arranged, they had met each other and courted for roughly a year before deciding to get married. She had liked Dinesh since the very beginning. He was tall, skinny, wore glasses and had a quiet manner. He was never overly affectionate but not withholding either. He didn't like to hold hands in public but he was always ready with a hug whenever she needed it. The fact that he was just a teacher didn't bother Seema. She made enough money for the both of them and Dinesh was more than happy staying home to do the housework. In any case, having lived alone in Delhi for years, he cooked better than Seema.

They had kissed on their fourth date but waited until they got married to have sex. Dinesh was a virgin, he confessed, and although Seema wasn't, she lied and said she was. She had had one serious boyfriend before, to whom she'd lost her virginity, but he hadn't been very good, always finishing within a minute or two. Dinesh was a good lover though, caring and considerate. And since it was only with Dinesh that she actually found herself enjoying sex, she considered him her first for all intents and purposes. Theirs was thus a relationship of calm. In their year and a half together, they rarely expected too much of the other and had come to accept everything about the other person. Seema was certain that she loved Dinesh dearly and she was just as certain that he did too.

So the kiss she had shared with Kaushal rested heavily on her mind, but not with enough weight to have her reconsider her marriage. She knew she was attracted to Kaushal but she expected these things to happen and for them to run their course. She had made a mistake by kissing him, but she was going to refrain from taking things any further. And there was really no point in telling Dinesh. It would only upset him, and what was the point of that if it was never going to happen again. Hand-holding was innocent, kids' stuff.

Her reassurances to herself aside, Kaushal did not stop pursuing her. He never seemed to lose hope and he never got upset either. Every day he was the same cheery, jokey, slightly annoying personality. It was as if nothing ever got to him. Even now, as Seema looked at him sitting across from her and sipping his tea, he seemed content.

Her tea was getting cold and she hadn't taken a single sip. Kaushal was talking but Seema was not listening. She looked past him and out the door of the tea shop, into the street. There was a man with an unfurled umbrella on the other side of the street. There were clouds in the sky but no sign of rain. The man raised his umbrella over his head and waited expectantly as Seema watched. Two pigeons, roosting under the eaves of a nearby shop, suddenly flew out and swooped low in an arc over the heads of pedestrians, neatly dropping twin payloads onto the waiting umbrella of the man. He lowered the umbrella, surveyed the droppings, and closed it. Seemingly satisfied, he turned and disappeared into the crowd.

'Are you even listening to me?'

Seema was startled.

'What is wrong with you today?' Kaushal asked, finally looking exasperated.

'I had an accident yesterday,' Seema said.

'What?' Kaushal was concerned.

'It wasn't anything major. I hit something. A dog, I think.'

'Oh no, did it die?'

'I think so.'

'Well, at least it died. It would've suffered if it had lived.'

'Don't say that.'

'Don't worry, Seema, it was just a dog. These things happen. There are thousands of stray dogs in the city. There's no point in being sad about it.'

'But I hit it.'

'Yes, but I'm sure you didn't do it on purpose. It was an accident. What were you doing anyway?'

She had been staring straight ahead on her way home from work. She had been listening to Narayan Gopal on the radio and she had been thinking. She had been thinking about Kaushal and how, earlier that day, he had casually put his arm around her waist and she had felt his hips against hers. She had been thinking about the nape of his neck, the hollow of his throat, the crook of his elbow, the tautness of his stomach and the hardness beneath.

'Nothing,' she blushed suddenly. 'I was just driving.'

They finished their tea and walked back to the office. Rojina gave Seema a knowing smile as she passed and Seema looked away uncomfortably. Everyone in the office knew Seema was married and everyone in the office knew how close Kaushal and Seema were. The only saving grace, Seema thought, was the fact that they bickered like siblings. Most seemed to assume that lovers act like lovers around each other, with long, lingering gazes, batting eyelashes, giggling shyly with a turning away of the head and a propensity to talk to each other in soft, adoring tones. In contrast, Kaushal and Seema yelled at each other, cursed each other and were constantly fighting.

City of Dreams

Seema got back to work but even her numbers seemed hostile to her. The sevens looked long and sharp, like outstretched knives, the threes looked like they were mocking her with their twin curves, the eights winked at her lewdly. She closed her eyes and tried to clear her mind. A low, steady roar reverberated through the office from the generator next door and the clacking of keyboards rose from all around her. Off to one end, someone was talking loudly on the phone and laughing from their gut. She forced herself to open her eyes.

She wanted to quit her job, she decided. This wasn't working out for her. She was sick of adding and subtracting and she was sick of writing proposals. She would march right up to her boss, one Ramesh Sharma, and tell him right now. She got up from her desk and looked towards Mr Sharma's room. The blinds were drawn so she couldn't see inside. She walked up to Rojina.

'Is Ramesh sir in?'

'Yes, but he's on the phone right now so don't go in,' Rojina said. 'What do you need?'

'I think I want to quit,' Seema said.

Rojina stared at her blankly.

'Sanchi, I can't work here anymore.'

'But...but why? You make good money and there's not much work to do. Are you serious?'

'I've had enough of budgeting and proposal writing.'

At that instant, Ramesh Sharma emerged from his room, coat slung over his back.

'Hello Seema,' he nodded in her direction. 'Rojina, I need to leave urgently.' He looked back at Seema. 'Are you okay?

You look sick.' And before Seema could respond, he was already striding away and out the door.

'Have you gone mad, Seema?' Rojina asked. '*Dimaag khuskyo ki kya ho?*'

Seema didn't respond, just walked silently back to her desk and sat down. She took off her heels and sat there barefoot. She closed the Excel spreadsheet and spent the rest of the day on Facebook, going over pictures of other people's children and other people's pets. All the while she felt as if a yawning chasm had opened up inside her that nothing, not even a child or a pet, could fill.

At the end of the day, as Seema prepared to leave, Kaushal offered her a ride home.

'I noticed you don't have your car today,' he said. 'Did the dog dent it?'

'No,' she replied. 'I just didn't feel like driving.'

'I'll drop you home then.'

'No, it's okay. I'm going to take the bus.'

'Come on, Seema, it's no problem. *Bato parcha.*'

Seema relented and got behind him on his Pulsar. She didn't particularly like motorbikes, but she didn't feel like braving rush hour on a packed microbus either. She didn't think she would be able to take the forced closeness of other people right now, especially strangers. Kaushal drove fast and Seema found herself holding onto his shoulders. By the time they crossed the Bagmati bridge, Seema's hands had found their way around his waist with her face against his back. She felt light-headed and clutched him tighter.

As Kaushal slowed down to turn towards Baluwatar from Lainchour, Seema whispered to keep going.

'What?' Kaushal turned his head.

'Keep going.'

'Keep going where?'

'Wherever.'

'What are you talking about?'

'Just keep going. I don't want to go home.'

Kaushal seemed bewildered but he complied, speeding up towards Chakrapath, where he lived. Seema closed her eyes and rested close against Kaushal's back. She could feel his muscles tense with every turn and relax with every overtake. The cold wind sent daggers against her cheeks and her hair flew free behind her out of its confining ponytail, but all she concentrated on was the warmth of Kaushal's body against hers.

At Kaushal's house they entered without a word. Kaushal took hold of Seema's hand and led her up a flight of stairs. Inside his room, he shut the door behind them and kissed her. Seema responded hungrily, their tongues sparring like boxers. The room was dark and she took off her clothes in the evening light, which was streaming in through gaps in the curtains. She jumped when his hands first met her bare skin, leaving a trail of goosebumps as they travelled over her body. In the dim light, she took in his lean, muscular body even as she held her arms crossed over her own plumpness. He lay her down on the bed and the moment he entered her, she thought she would die. She stared up into the gloom, at the ceiling with a hand clamped over her mouth to stop from screaming. There was a hanging lightbulb and she stared fixedly at it, digging her nails into Kaushal's back. The one lightbulb hung and swung from the ceiling and then there were two lightbulbs and they were both swinging, then three and then a hundred, mad and lurching, beating and blurring, pounding and pulsating. She bit into her own palm hard enough to draw blood and watched mutely as Kaushal finished on her stomach.

'I don't want to go home,' she said after what seemed like an eternity.

'You can stay here,' Kaushal offered.

'Can we do this again?' she asked.

'Give me fifteen minutes.'

They spent all night in bed. Kaushal left the room a few times to go to the bathroom and get water. Seema barely moved. She did not take charge nor make any demands. She responded to all of Kaushal's advances, but as if dissociated from herself. She watched herself mutely when Kaushal climbed off her and when he turned her on her knees. But when he tried to turn on the lights, she screamed at him to stop and they lay there in the dark, not talking. Kaushal tried to make conversation but Seema would not respond. All she asked was, 'Again?'

Seema heard her phone buzzing the first five times. After that, there were no more calls. By the time she fell asleep, it was long past midnight.

They woke up sticky and sweaty but that did not seem to matter to Seema. She kissed Kaushal open-mouthed before he could even open his eyes. When Kaushal asked if she would like to shower and eat breakfast, she refused.

'I'm not going to work,' she said.

'You have to go to work.'

'Who says I have to do anything?'

'Then you should go home.'

'Why? Because my buda might be worried?'

'...'

'*Ta jaa*, you go to work.'

'And just leave you here?"

'Yes.'

'But I can't just leave you here.'

'I promise not to steal anything.'

'It's not that. What're you going to do here? What are you going to eat?'

'I'll manage.'

'Seema, you're acting really strange.'

'You didn't think anything was strange last night.'

'...'

'Please, just leave me alone.'

Kaushal left for work, anxious and afraid. Seema lay in Kaushal's bed for a long time, staring up at that single lightbulb. She took a cold shower, washing all of last night and this morning off of her body. She stood unflinching as the cold water struck her like a hail of gunfire. When she was ready, she left and walked all the way home.

At the gate, Dinesh was distraught. 'Where were you last night? I called you a thousand times. I called the police. I was really worried. What's going on?'

'You called me five times, Dinesh.'

'Are you okay? Where were you?'

'It doesn't matter.'

'Were you with someone else? I can smell shampoo.'

'I cheated on you, Dinesh,' Seema said monotonously, as if reciting lines she's repeated a thousand times before. 'We should get a divorce.'

'What?' Dinesh only stared at her. She was wearing yesterday's clothes, all crumpled and creased. Her hair was wet and loose, coming down in a cascade.

Seema kept walking into the house, past Dinesh, past the car that her father had bought for her as a wedding present and into the house that Dinesh's parents had set aside for his marriage. She walked to her room and lay prostrate on the bed, unmoving. Dinesh was talking, yelling and crying all at the same time. She couldn't hear him. Her mind was far, far away.

She was thinking of that evening in her car, driving with Narayan Gopal singing 'Ma Ta Laligurans Bhayechu' on the radio. She had been fantasizing, her fingers tapping absently on the steering wheel. The flash of movement had been sudden and the thud oh so loud. She knew before she even looked in the rear-view mirror. She had expected an angry horde to descend and tear her to pieces, beat her and burn her in her car. Maybe that would have been kinder. She had looked at the mirror and, in the evening, against the empty expanse of the street, the body had looked so small, so fragile and so alone.

She made her choice. One voice turning off and another voice turning on.

'It's just a dog,' the voice said.

Acknowledgements

I must thank my mother and brother, without whom I wouldn't be the person I am today.

Also my extended family, my grandparents, my uncles and aunts, especially Thulomua, who has been a rock during very hard times.

And my cousins—growing up with you has been quite the adventure.

Those who, for some strange unfathomable reason, have refused to give up on me and my writing—Prateebha, Shu Yun, Tiku, Ayushma.

Avinesh—cousin, friend and confidante.

All of my friends who've provided me so readily, and so unwittingly, with so much material, especially Ramesh, Kushal, Salil, the Chakrapath boys.

My buddy Tom, with whom I've had conversations on just about everything under the sun.

Anu, who once saved my life.

Friend Atul Thakur, without whom this book might not have been published.

My former bosses, Kunda and Akhilesh, who taught me much about the ways of the world, and especially Anagha, who hammered me and my writing into shape.

My teachers, all the way from Sundar Gurung and Dhiraj Gurung to Milan Dixit and Perry Thapa to Una Chung and Rona Mark. Everything you taught me made me a more interesting writer.

Rupa Publications for taking a chance on me, Anurag for the initial edit and Dharini for everything else.

Prawin, Rabi and Pranab for helping me with the ins and outs of publishing.

Samrat Upadhyay for reading a short story so long ago and giving me feedback.

And everyone I've ever loved, you know who you are.